Shadow of the Grizzly

LARRY JAY MARTIN

Shadow of the Grizzly

A Double D Western
DOUBLEDAY
New York London Toronto Sydney Auckland

A Double D Western
PUBLISHED BY DOUBLEDAY
a division of Bantam Doubleday Dell Publishing Group, Inc.
1540 Broadway, New York, New York 10036

Double D Western, Doubleday,
and the portrayal of the letters DD
are trademarks of Doubleday, a division of
Bantam Doubleday Dell Publishing Group, Inc.

Library of Congress Cataloging-in-Publication Data

Martin, Larry Jay.
Shadow of the grizzly/Larry Jay Martin.—1st ed.
    p.   cm.—(A Double D western)
1. Grizzly bear—Fiction. I. Title.
PS3563.A72487S5   1993
813′.54—dc20   92-37878
CIP

ISBN 0-385-46902-0
Copyright © 1993 by Larry Jay Martin
All Rights Reserved
Printed in the United States of America
May 1993
First Edition

10 9 8 7 6 5 4 3 2 1

This novel is dedicated to all the species—
the proud, the humble, the beautiful,
and in weak human eyes, the not-so-beautiful—
that have been doomed by man,
with great testimony to his ignorance,
and particularly to the subspecies Californicus
of Ursus Arctos Horribilis

The last magnificent California grizzly was killed
in Tulare County, near the setting of this novel, in 1921

One

QUIETLY, moving with stealth in spite of his great size, the huge boar silvertip shouldered its way down the chaparral-covered hillside, then paused, unmoving as the granite rocks nearby.

Watchful eyes, small as a pig's but not so keen, studied a boy as he approached a wide clearing where a sandspit stretched along the sycamore-and-live-oak-lined river. But then the massive animal's attention shifted to others, running back and forth in seeming confusion on the open field.

The silent watcher had no way of knowing the boy making his way through the underbrush was the son of Trokhud, a Yocuts chieftain, or *capitán* as the Mexicans preferred calling a tribal headman. The boy was in his twelfth summer and big for his age. His name was Wehaysit, for even as a knee-high youngster he was as brave as the tawny mountain lion he was named for. And he was proud of his name, of his skill at hunting, and of his skill at games.

They had gathered in a wide sand field just across the Tule River from the village, the place the young and old congregated to play the game, *kahdah duich,* or Shinny, as the few whites in the wide marshy Ton Tache, or San Joaquin, Valley called it. But only the young gathered to play that afternoon, for the elders were on an antelope drive. Much to his chagrin, Wehaysit had been ordered by his mother to stay at home and snare pigeons. She was far more sure of his chance at success at snaring than she was of having a young antelope for the pot that night—and the family must be fed. As requested, Wehaysit had staked out his pet pigeon, spread some tiny black doveweed seed, and the feeding bird had attracted others. Concealed in a brush-blind, the slender dark-skinned and raven-haired boy had deftly jerked the hand noose, and by mid-morning had four spring-fat birds for the pot.

Then he could turn his attention to other things.

When Wehaysit had turned ten, his father had given him his first *kahdah duich* club. Formed carefully from a sapling with a natural crook at its base, lovingly whittled and shaped while green, dried, then hardened by fire, it might have been mistaken for the white man's hockey club, for it too had a crooked end and a fine rawhide woven handle.

His mother, Kayyah, thinner-faced and finer-featured than most Yocuts women, had smiled and sent him on his way when he brought the pigeons so early into the willow and tule reed hut. The family resided in a riverside village of two dozen such structures—many of them forty paces long with common walls providing for many families. With a smile and glance of motherly pride, she told him he could go ahead and join his friends and play the game.

Still, he would have rather been with the men on the antelope drive.

A dozen boys, most smaller than Wehaysit, were hard at play, batting a wooden ball formed from a hard oak burl. The object was to drive the ball to their respective goal, a hole in the ground. It was no easy task, as the goals were four hundred paces apart across the soft sand, and the swinging of opposing clubs viciously barred passage.

Each Yocuts village lay in the center of a watershed, and by ancient agreement no Yocuts would hunt in the territory of another village across distant ridges, in the next waterway. The Tule River flowed from high in the Sierra Nevada to the east, beginning to collect and run westward on hard-edged granite slopes above the timber line, joining to form creeks in high fern-covered, redwood-shaded meadows, then joining again, becoming full-fledged streams growing in volume as they cascaded through spruce and cedar and pine forest. Finally they merged with other creeks and streams and became, at last, the river. In deep ravines lined with dusky digger pine and sandpaper oak, the water wound its way over and around smooth river rock under plumes of white blossoms spotting the dark green foliage of buckeye. Occasionally it flowed quietly, only to awake in turbulent tumbles of white water, dashing over and around granite impediments.

Those same waters nurtured the deer of the pine-, spruce-, and cedar-covered sub-alpine, then the elk, antelope, and deer of the oak- and digger-pine-covered lower hills, or piedmont, and then the great varieties of birds and animals of the wide marshy valley. Coyote, wolf, bobcat, and cougar preyed on both large and small, and badger, skunk, raven, turkey vulture, and condor fed on the carrion they left.

In the high mountains, foothills, and marshy valley, all creatures —including humans—moved quickly aside for the god the Yocuts knew as *mohoo*. Even seeing his massive fur-covered bulk at great distance would pound the heart and wet the palms.

The grizzly ruled, king of the land and all living things, king of even the heavens to the Yocuts. The god, *mohoo*.

All California lived in the shadow of the grizzly.

And the great bear treated even man with disdain, unless he was wounded or sick and unable to find the berries, pine nuts, and clover, or small rodents he normally fed upon.

Twotoes rose high on his hind legs, lifting his six hundred pounds to his full nine-foot height to study the scene a hundred paces below. A flurry of activity was underway on the wide sand bar separating the underbrush from the creek. The foul smell of man lay everywhere and Twotoes shook his head and snorted to clear his nostrils of it. And worse, the man-animals below carried sticks. Sticks not unlike those that had spit fire and smoke at him, fire and smoke that still scorched his insides.

Normally he would have avoided the smell of man, a smell that had offended him only a few days before when three of the creatures, along with a dozen wolf-like beasts, had invaded the quiet of his lodgepole pine thicket in the high mountains. The first time he had encountered the smell was before the snows had come, and then only on the trap that had ripped three of the outside toes from his left forefoot—then he had not seen the source of the bad smell, but had associated it with that paw-wrenching pain.

This last time the men had come, after the snow left, behind dogs. He had not moved away then, refusing to give ground to these interlopers, but the dogs had harried him back and forth through the stand of pine where he often bedded down. Even though he easily disemboweled three of the dogs and crippled two more, the men, and the sticks they carried, had spit the fire and smoke at him and he had been dizzy with the pain of it since. Only then, wounded and bleeding, did he run, leaving his stand of lodgepoles to the men and dogs. Still, deep in his insides the pain cried out to him—sometimes a low keen, sometimes a scream.

While lying for days under western red cedar, amid aromatic bear clover, high on a mountain side where he could see his back trail for miles, he had licked the wounds on his side and right foreleg until they were healed, but still the fiery worm gnawed deep at his middle. The cedar slope had been a healing place, with a trickle of ice-cold water to drink, but it had only partially done its job.

Since then he had roamed lower and lower in the mountains. His foreleg did not work so well, and he could not climb as he once had. Dropping in elevation, he found fewer and fewer berries and pine nuts, and could not catch the ground squirrels and mice as he could not move quickly enough—for each time he tried his head swam and his gut wrenched with pain.

He had been living on grasses and clover, tearing open rotten logs with his razor-sharp two-inch claws, looking for termites— eating only out of instinct, for he had no appetite and was losing weight daily.

He needed meat. It required far too many termites to fill his great six-hundred-pound body.

And these creatures below, moving back and forth in confusion, were the sustenance he needed.

The boy, Wehaysit, yelled to one of the players and asked how many were on each team, then joined the one with the fewest. As one of the largest players, he soon had the burl and was off to his goal, pursued by the swinging clubs of his teammates and opponents. He scored easily and they returned the burl to the center of the field, laughing and puffing with the exhaustion of the run.

The burl was dropped in the middle, and the two teams backed away—then all the players drove forward and formed a melee of bodies and swinging clubs until the ball popped free over to the uphill side of the field. Wehaysit led the pack, caught up with the ball, slapping it toward his goal, then turned to pursue it. The others, following closely, yelling in delight, stopped in sudden wide-eyed fear just as Wehaysit spun to face them. The silence caused Wehaysit to halt in his tracks and turn back—just in time to see the massive form rumble out of the underbrush, mouth slavering, muscles bunched as the monster closed the few steps between them.

Wehaysit thrust his club in front of him, trying vainly to ward off the charging mass of snarling muscle. He turned to run—but the bear was on him, enveloping him. Teeth closed on the back of Wehaysit's neck, the sound of snapping bone rang across the field, and his head canted at an odd angle and his eyes rolled back.

Almost before they could turn in panic, the other boys saw their friend snatched from the field and dragged, flopping like a dying bird, back into the chaparral.

They hesitated and watched in morbid terror, knowing that there was nothing they or anyone in the village could do against the great god *mohoo*.

The remaining players had to cross the river to get to the village, screaming in fright, splashing, falling, and were met by its women. One of the boys ran on to Wehaysit's family hut, and puffing and crying told Kayyah of her son's fate.

Carrying a stone pestle, a useless weapon, she ran for the river, crossed it and the field, and followed the track of the bear—great fourteen-inch indentations in the soft earth under the chaparral. And an occasional splatter of blood.

She climbed the hill in the thick brush until she fell in exhaustion, her chest heaving in gasps of desire—want of air, and of the return of her child.

She quieted, rose to a sitting position, then wrapped her arms tightly around herself and began to rock back and forth—and to wail.

That too was for naught.

Her keening still pierced the quiet air from high on the hillside when her husband Trokhud returned at dusk, an antelope proudly draped across his shoulders. He was told of his son's fate, and he laid the antelope aside, unimportant now. He did not have to follow the trail of great bear tracks and the drag marks of his son's body up the steep brush-covered hillside to find his wife.

Wails of lament led him to her.

Two

JOHN CLINTON RYAN had picked a wide live-oak-and-syca-more-covered flat, much like that of the Yocuts' Tule River village, to build his rancho headquarters. But this spot had several offshoots of the main river channel, natural irrigation ditches that fed the fields. In many places the flats and trees lay lushly covered with wild grapes and berry vines, and the meadows stood shoulder-deep in grass. He had stumbled on this spot on the Kaweah River on the east side of the great Ton Tache Valley while making his own trail north from Pueblo de Los Angeles a year before, and had become completely enamored of the luxuriant beauty and richness of it.

After the California Revolution, when the Anglos dispossessed the Mexicans of the government and much of their lands, Ryan had found himself out of work in Pueblo de Los Angeles. Out of work, but with a good horse, an Andalusian palomino he called Diablo del Sol, Sun Devil, a pack mule, two fine .36 caliber Navy Colts, a pair of .31 caliber Allen pepperboxes, a .50 caliber Hawken rifle, and a ten-shot revolving-breech .36 caliber Colt's rifle. The latter had served him well during the California Revolution.

More important, he possessed a knowledge of the land—at least the California coast and the hills of California south of Los Angeles. After a life at sea, he now found that he could live off the land. A skilled older *vaquero* had taken him under wing and taught him the ways of horses and cattle, and finally of bear, cougar, and the back country. Now he could set a snare with the best of them, and knew to follow a bee or dove to water. So, with little trepidation, he had set out north into the country few men knew anything about, across the high mountains north of Pueblo de Los Angeles until the wide valley opened before him.

Every few miles as he had made his way, alone except for Diablo and the mule, along the foothills of the Sierras on the east side of the valley, he came across a free-flowing stream or river, a few so wide and deep that he had to swim the stock across. On his right rose the great Sierra Nevada, on his left spread a valley of tule marsh in the low spots and chaparral rises where the flat swelled high enough out of the water courses to stand dry. The low hills, *lomarías,* and the tules were spotted with huge live oaks.

Indians occupied villages every few miles, living off the natural bounty of the land. No white men occupied the most southerly area of the valley, and he saw none as he traveled north—until he reached the trails to the gold fields.

He had heard a few tales of the great central valley from vaqueros who had chased horse-stealing Indians there from the coast, and had gone to the edge one time himself, also chasing a stolen horse herd, riding from Santa Barbara into the very southwest corner of the Ton Tache. But the trip north from Pueblo de Los Angeles had been the first time he had ever really seen it. And few other white men had. From Sacramento he had turned west and made his way to San Francisco Bay, and finally across it on a work scow to the burgeoning city itself.

But always, while he worked in the city, he had wanted to make his way back to the river the Indians called Kaweah. Back to the giant live oaks and sycamore, with the great hard-shouldered granite mountains rising to the east and the valley spreading to the west.

Deer, elk, and antelope filled the foothills and the valley. Ducks, geese, swans, pelicans, sand hill and whooping cranes, and a thousand other varieties of waterfowl moved up and down the valley with the seasons. The streams and lakes lay filled with fish; salmon ran many of the rivers.

And make his way back he did. Dealing with a Yocuts chief and the village elders, he negotiated a treaty where he would occupy the land south of the Kaweah. He would ranch, and the Indians would continue to hunt and gather. Two dozen horses had been delivered to the Yocuts to seal the bargain—horses that would be eaten, not ridden. It was the Yocuts' way, now that the Mexicans had introduced the horse to their country. They had become dependent upon the horse as their staple; no longer was the acorn the primary food. Clint spent hours making them understand that he would be bringing horses to raise for riding; that *his* horses were special—not to be eaten.

And he had changed the land, at least some of it. He had brought cattle and horses and hogs and sheep, for the grass lay belly-deep, the water plentiful, and the winters mild.

And he loved every hour of it. He had been tired of people—at least city people.

Clint leaned against the clean barked rail of the new breaking pen, watching Ramón give Gideon a lesson in horse breaking. Built for strength, the pen, except for its gate, was constructed of posts buried upright, side by side, a solid wall of outward-leaning logs. The subject of Ramón's attention was a dun-colored, Roman-nosed broomtail that was not among the forty original Andalusians he had received for helping Don Carlos Vega. A few wild horses ran free in the tules, and this broomtail had been chased by Clint right into Ramón's *reata*. The broomtail was a kicker, and Ramón wanted to cure that as well as break the animal to hobbles. He had the broomtail's right forefoot and left hindfoot tied together, and the left forefoot and right hindfoot rather close together. The rawhide lines formed an X under the horse. Each time the dun tried to kick, he tumbled to his side in the corral dust—and Ramón let him lie there for twenty minutes and consider the consequences of his bad habit. Again the dun kicked with his right rear hoof and again he tumbled to the dust, his left forefoot jerked out from under him. Ramón and Gideon ambled over to the gate rail where Clint had climbed to watch.

"You have nothing better to do," Ramón chided, wiping his

dark-skinned brow, furrowed from years of age, wind, and sun, "than watch this poor excuse for a *caballo* be taught manners?"

"Been cutting corral posts," Clint answered with a crooked smile covering his much lighter—although sun-darkened—face, "and my back convinced my legs to wander over and watch you two teach that knothead to stand quiet."

Gideon, darker than either of them, with tightly curled black hair, mounted the gate rail beside him. "Ramón got tired of watchin' me lose the kickin' contest. When's the dinner bell?" he asked. He shaded onyx black eyes with a callused hand as he glanced up at the sun high overhead.

"I don't know," Clint said, his own stomach beginning to complain. He doffed his hat and ran his hand through an ample mane of fair hair, then centered warm green eyes—eyes that became cold and blue as pond ice when he or his was threatened—on Gideon, who sat equally tall on the gate rail. "I saw little Billy out gathering wild onions a while ago and took that for a good sign. Maybe his old man has whipped up a stew from that deer you shot yesterday."

"Or better yet," Gideon said as he jumped down from the rail, "maybe ol' Gordy's roasted one of those sand hill cranes Ramón shot."

"You two *gringos*"—to Ramón even a black man like Gideon was an interloping gringo—"are making me hungry just listening to you. More than likely, Gordy has beans and corn mush. . . . What he is best at."

"True," Clint said. "Let's wash up and find out."

The piece of metal hanging from the ranch house eave began to clang.

"My gut's a better timepiece, least when it comes to dinner, than old Seth Thomas ever made," Gideon said with a laugh, and sprang over the rails in an easy motion.

"You two would let this fine animal lie here for the buzzards," Ramón said, hurrying to untie the dun.

"No we wouldn't," Clint yelled back over his shoulder. "But

we knew damn well *you* wouldn't. . . . You're getting old and soft, vaquero."

"Do not confuse age with softness, gringo," Ramón said sagely. "The devil is not the devil because he is the devil, but because he is old."

Clint and Gideon chuckled as they hurried to wash up for dinner, leaving the older man to care for the horse. They knew he would complain if they tried to do a lick of his work.

Four others shared Clint's ranch, Rancho Kaweah, with him.

Ramón Diego had taught Clint the use of *romal*, reata, and *bosal* when Clint had first landed in California, and there was no man better with horses. When Clint had managed to earn forty prime head of Andalusians to stock the ranch, he had sent for Ramón straight away. For what was a horse and cattle ranch without a *caballero*—and Ramón María Diego, even with a well-furrowed face and hair now highlighted with gray, was the best in the land. A man with hatchet features, Ramón could be as cold, quick, and deadly efficient as that implement.

Gideon LaMont was black, big—equally tall as Clint and more thickchested—and smooth and fast as quicksilver. Big doe eyes occasionally grew warm as a cup of fresh coffee, until flattened cold-black by anger. Gideon was a freedman, by fate, for his former master had been shot and killed in San Francisco while Clint looked on. Clint had helped Gideon, who suddenly found himself free for the first time in his life and surrounded by the craziness of burgeoning San Francisco, and been in turn helped by him. They had been friends ever since. Gideon was a willing worker who had spent his early life on a New Orleans plantation, and he knew how to build a mill, lay out a water ditch, de-hair a hog, make sausage, or do a thousand other things that would set Rancho Kaweah apart from the normal *Californio* rancho.

William Gordon Jessup had been in Stockton, dead broke and hungry, when Clint and Gideon had passed through heading south to the Kaweah. He didn't have a stake and needed work. Clint agreed to hire him for a dollar a day and found, and give him one day a week to go prospecting. He had softened to the man's plight because Gordy had his son with him, and the boy was hungry too. Clint never could abide a hungry child, for it reminded him of his own past. Gordy stood shorter than Clint or Gideon, but was built like a tree trunk with thick forearms and legs, and fingers like corn cobs. Curly blond hair, the same sandy shade as that on his head, covered his chest and arms, and he studied you with intense blue eyes. It always amazed Clint that the man had been able to do the fine work of a jeweler—his eastern profession —with those stubby fingers.

Billy Jessup was a wisp of a whip-thin eleven-year-old boy, blond and freckled, blue-eyed, eager and watching, wanting to know everything. His mother had died of yellow fever on the trip around the Horn, and Gordy seemed at a complete loss about what to do with the boy.

Clint Ryan kept seeing himself in the blond boy.

As a child of only seven, Clint had been indentured to a tanner —a hard man—after Clint's parents and a sister had died from the fever on the trip over from Ireland. Had it not been for seeing Billy, Gordy's son, hollow-eyed with lack of food, clinging to his father, Clint would have refused to hire the man, for Gordy had been a jeweler in Boston and had few skills of use to a rancho. And he did have a madness to find the yellow metal that he had used so often in his craft, a dependent son that precluded him from pursuing it, and a growing frustration that he was required to do anything else.

As they suspected, Gordy Jessup had the table set with tin plates and centered with a bowl of beans and a bowl of stewed corn. Biscuits and a few slivers of fried sidepork on a platter saved him from a dressing-down by the other three men. When it had been discovered that he had few ranch skills, but had been forced after the loss of his wife to learn the rudiments of the kitchen, Gordy had been immediately recruited to the stove-end of the long one-room logpole house that served as ranch headquarters. Clint was teaching him the curing of meat in the only other building on the ranch, which was a combination slaughterhouse, *matanza*, and log smokehouse.

When Clint had first made his way back to the Kaweah and realized how many acorns the oak thickets beyond the river held, he immediately returned north, purchased, and drove down a small herd of swine. In the months the animals had been at the ranch, the herd had already doubled. The initial investment had been a big one, thirty dollars a head for two dozen—many not much more than shoats themselves. The gold rush up north had driven prices high.

But if trends held, Clint's horses, cattle—many of which he had gathered wild out of the tules—and swine would bring unbelievably high prices. Meat was at a premium in the gold fields. He also had a herd of sheep grazing in the nearby foothills, tended by an Indian he had trained to follow the grass, though he had lost half the sixty he had started with to wolves, coyotes, and, he feared, to other Indians, before the man had become adept at his job.

Little Billy Jessup took a seat next to Clint as he always tried to do.

"When are you gonna let me pick out a horse to ride, Mr. Ryan?" Billy asked.

"Don't you be pestering Mr. Ryan," his father snapped, and Billy quieted immediately.

Clint finished gnawing a bite of sidepork before he spoke. "It's natural for a boy to want to ride, Gordy." He turned to the boy and ruffled his blond hair. "As soon as your father says it's alright, we'll pick you out a gentle one and if you hold your mouth just right, you might even talk ol' Ramón into makin' you a saddle and bridle."

"He will make his own," Ramón said quietly, without looking up from his plate.

Billy looked a little confused. "How do I have to 'hold my mouth'?"

Clint chuckled. "I'll let you work that out with Ramón, Billy me lad."

"You do your chores," Ramón added, "and I'll help you make a saddle and become a fine *trenzadoro.*"

"*Tren . . . tren . . .* What's that, Mr. Diego?"

"Braider, boy. You will be able to braid your own reins and *romal* and *bosal* and reata, and weave a fine horsehair *cincha.*"

Billy gave the vaquero a grateful look, flashed a smile at Clint, then an apprehensive look at his father. The look he got in return made him return his attention to his plate.

The rest of the meal was spent discussing the upcoming project —the building of the *establo,* or barn. Gideon wanted to build it all out of logs with a hayloft. Ramón, on the other hand, wanted it single story, from adobe, with a tile roof. It was an argument, albeit a good-natured one, that had begun almost as soon as the two men had met. Gideon pushed for things to be done as they had been on the plantations of New Orleans, where he hailed from, and Ramón wanted to do things in the old Californio way.

As they chided each other, the clunk of a stone hitting planks turned all heads that way.

"Must be ol' Chahchabe," Clint said, rising and heading for the door. Chahchabe was the head of the Kaweah Yocuts tribe. The Yocuts seldom came to call, and when they did, always stood back a polite distance and chucked a rock at the door.

But when he opened the door, the Indians who stood a respectable distance away were none he had seen before.

"Don't know these fellows," Clint cautioned over his shoulder before he started out.

Ramón and Gideon walked to their respective bunks and picked up their rifles, checking the loads before following Clint out. They did not carry the weapons with them, but leaned them close by against the wall. The Indians in the area had caused them no trouble, though they had heard of plenty of Indian problems in other areas of California. Billy started out behind them.

"Billy," his father warned, and the boy stopped short. Instead, he went to one of the two windows in the front side of the house, and watched from there.

Clint crossed the barren yard and greeted the half-dozen Indians. The Yocuts had carrying nets slung over their shoulders, and had been gathering as they journeyed. Berries and herbs, acorns and nuts filled the nets. Low waisted and heavily limbed, each man was armed with a bow and half a dozen two-foot-long headless shafts. In a carrying pouch on their waist rode a variety of foreshafts that fitted tightly onto the shafts. Special arrowheads for birds and rabbits, as well as for bigger game, could be interchanged. Most of the men carried a stone knife as part of their coiled hairstyle. Barefoot, they were clad only in rabbit skin loincloths, as the weather was mild.

Clint bade them sit, and they all did so in a circle in the dirt yard in front of the house, then he yelled to Gordy to bring what was left of the corn, beans, and biscuits.

Ramón joined them, since he knew some of the language of the Chumash, the coastal Indians who resided near Santa Barbara, and a few words of it and the Yocuts language were the same. Between the signing and Ramón's few words, they soon discovered that the man who seemed to be in charge was Trokhud, a thick-shouldered man with short legs, and the others were elders from a tribe three days' walk to the south.

And they had a problem.

A grizzly had come and taken the son of the chief, and he wanted revenge—much to the displeasure of the other elders. The grizzly bear, Ramón explained, was sacred to the Yocuts.

Trokhud argued that this bear would be easy to find, for he had lost three toes on his left forefoot.

Clint listened politely, wondering what he could do. The Indians explained that they had no weapon to fight the bear, but Clint and his men did. They wanted Clint and the others to hunt the bear with their rifles.

Clint sighed deeply. He had a ranch to run. He had a list of projects as long as his arm, many of which he had no idea how to accomplish much less find the time to do so. The last thing he needed was a hunting trip.

He walked the Indians to a pleasant spot in a sycamore grove downriver a hundred paces, showed them he wanted them to camp there, and returned to the house. He would give them an answer after he slept on it.

They worked the day out, then gathered again with the Yocuts. Ramón and Gideon had spent the early afternoon killing and preparing a shoat for the fire, Gordy had turned it over the coals for the last hours, and by day's end, it, and beans, squash, corn, and several dozen of Ramón's misshapen but flavorful tortillas, graced the plank table that had been carried out into the yard and placed under a wide live oak. The Indians added berries, wild rose hips, and watercress collected from the riverside.

The evening was filled with goodwill.

But that night, Clint could not sleep. He tossed and turned and tried to reconcile not helping the Yocuts—and in his dreams, when he did sleep, he was haunted by a bear with three missing toes.

It was critical he maintain the goodwill of the natives, but these were Indians from far away. Hell, he could find himself doing nothing but resolving Indian problems, and the barn would never be built and a hundred other projects never started. True, he had guns, but the Indians had been getting along for hundreds . . . thousands of years without his guns or anyone else's.

And he had things to do.

Finally, he fell into a fitful sleep, awaking before the sun, feeling far less than rested. He arose and walked to the river and took a quick dip as the sun colored the eastern sky over the mountains. Before the others awoke, he walked to the site of the barn and paced it off for the hundredth time, restacking the rocks that marked its corners.

They would begin the *establo* today, not after some hunt for a bear that was probably already across the mountains—mountains where the sun was just beginning to form a line of silver.

He walked to the Indian camp, and though feeling a twinge of guilt since he had always helped friends and neighbors when he could, he informed them he could not do what they asked. They left without ceremony, but Clint knew that the chief, Trokhud—dour and refusing to meet Clint's eyes—was terribly disappointed.

Clint returned to the ranch house, where Gordy was fixing breakfast, beans and bacon again, and flopped down at the plank table to sip a tin cup of coffee.

"Your coffee tastes like pig dung this morning," he groused at Gordy.

"And a good morning to you, too, Mr. Ryan," Gordy said. He ran a hand though his thinning blond hair and mopped the sweat away from his red-splotched brow, without turning from the iron stove. "It's getting too hot to cook inside. We'll need to be moving this stove out in the yard for it to be tolerable."

"You'll need a lean-to. Eventually we'll build a real *cocina*," Clint suggested, knowing that the heat of summer would soon be on them, and moving the stove outside was a good idea. The Californio ranchos had a separate kitchen building, *cocina*, apart from the house because of both the heat and the risk of fire. "But we're starting the barn today, and it'll have to wait."

"I'll build it myself if you'll cut a few extra poles."

"Good enough," Clint said, a little surprised and pleased that Gordy was showing the initiative.

"Tomorrow is my day off," Gordy said, still not turning from the stove.

"It's Sunday, I guess," Clint said.

"I'd like to head up in the hills after dinner today to try for some color in a few streams. I'll make supper up ahead of time and Billy can get it on the table."

Clint bit his lip, saying nothing. Gideon and Ramón stomped the dust off their boots, then ambled into the ranch house, breaking the silence.

"I saw you out tramping around the barn site this morning," Ramón said. "We are going to get started on it?"

"Soon as you put away these vittles."

"Adobe or wood?" Gideon asked.

"We've got enough adobe bricks made already," Clint said, eyeing the two men and noting the triumphant look growing on

Ramón's face. "So we'll build . . . the first floor out of adobe and the second out of logs."

"*¡Caramba!*" Ramón said, then filled his mouth with a biscuit. "She will look the half-breed, an *establo mestizo,*" he mumbled with a full mouth.

"With a hayloft?" Gideon asked.

"With a hayloft," Clint confirmed.

Billy arrived from the water trough, his hair still dripping where he'd slicked it back. "I can help," he offered enthusiastically.

"You've got to get the supper on," Gordy snapped at the boy. "I'm headin' for the hills this afternoon." He cut his eyes at Clint, who said nothing, neither affirming nor denying the request. If it wasn't for Billy, he would tell Gordy to just keep on going once he reached the hills.

"Can I help until then?" Billy asked Clint.

"We couldn't do it without you, Billy boy," Clint said, and ruffled the boy's matted blond hair.

Clint rose and stretched, having cleaned his plate. He looked to Gordy as he headed for the door. "Color your pan up with a hundred pounds of that yellow stuff so you can send this boy to a fine school in the Sandwich Islands."

Later, Clint glanced up from his work to see Gordy ride out, a pack horse behind him. Clint thought that strange, as all Gordy needed to prospect the low hills was a short-handled shovel and the gold pan he had brought from Stockton, not a pack horse full of supplies.

That next morning, they laid the foundation blocks for the barn.

Twotoes worked his way north in the low foothills, then, feeling much stronger, climbed high and followed a long ridge of blue granite until the weather cooled with the elevation and the deep shade of pines. He rested in a patch of manzanita, dozing and watching his back trail, his stomach heavy with meat.

He lay with his head on his forepaws, the view of the canyon below slowly getting better as the sun rose. A doe with twin fawns walked into a meadow, but hardly attracted Twotoes' interest as the gnats began to buzz around his eyes. He closed them, content for the first time in two weeks. The pain in his stomach was almost gone and his right foreleg felt close to normal.

Finally, he sensed something and opened his eyes. Raising to a sitting position, his forelegs extended, his rear legs still tucked under him, he eyed the meadow.

A cinnamon-colored sow grizzly with a dark cub wandered into the meadow; the doe and her fawns bolted away. Something deep in his small brain told him this sow was familiar, but he knew better than to approach her now. Even if he had no evil intent toward the cub, she would meet him with a full charge to protect the little miniature of herself.

No, he would be content to lie in the shade of the manzanita and watch. The gnats pestered him again, and again he closed his eyes.

When he was not much larger than the cub below, a big boar grizzly he recognized as Scarlip, the largest and most aggressive of the many bears in the high country, wandered near where he and his mother browsed. At first she paid the big boar little attention. But his mother did not hesitate when Scarlip moved into the berry patch where she and Twotoes foraged. Though much smaller, she charged him in a roaring run, and to both their surprise, knocked the bigger Scarlip rolling.

Pride injured, the bigger bear responded with a vengeance, and the female was no match for him. Fight as she may, teeth and claws making desperate cuts at the big boar, soon he had turned her and found the fatal grip on the back of her neck. Little Twotoes was standing on his hind legs, trying to see over the berry bushes, when Scarlip shook his head one final time. He turned the sow loose—and she fell unmoving into the meadow grass. Scarlip did not hesitate. He spun and charged into the berry bush after the small cub. Twotoes turned and ran as he had never run before. Out of the berry patch, over a small creek. Scarlip was on him. A powerful swipe of a forepaw sent him rolling up against a rock pile.

The panicked cub turned to run again, and found himself deep in a rock cleft. The big bear, his lips badly healed from a former fight—thus his name—made a fearful sight as he tried his best to reach Twotoes, who cowered as deeply in the cool dark cleft as he could retreat. Scarlip swung paws with claws like two-inch razors, flinging dirt, but not reaching him.

Trembling, his pounding heart yearning for his mother, the cub stayed in the cool protective haven of the rocks long after the big boar tired of the chase and left.

Finally, in the dark of a cold moonless night, he made his way out of the crack, across the berry patch, and into the meadow. He stopped and lapped water from a trickle and fed on some fresh clover, then continued. At last, he came upon the great brown heap of unmoving fur that smelled like his mother, but didn't respond.

He curled against her and slept.

He was awakened by the yipping of coyotes. He watched them circle, catching their smell more than the actual sight of them in the darkness. Surprised that his mother did not rise and send them scattering with one of her low growls, he tried himself. But his meager effort did little, and soon the boldest of the pack charged in. The little bear scampered around to the other side where another coyote was snarling and tearing at his mother's hind leg. Twotoes drove the animal away. But another charged in and nipped at his hocks, and when he spun to face that one, another raced forward.

Eventually, he found himself again being chased over the berry patch and into the fissure in the rocks.

He stayed there until morning, then ventured out again. This time, a mountain lion stood over the carcass of his mother and, trembling, Twotoes immediately retreated to the cleft.

By nightfall, his stomach gnawed at him. He found his way back to the berry patch and fed there. He stayed in the crack of the rocks off and on for weeks until he could no longer fit. Then he wandered away, seeking another source of food other than the diminishing berries. Nothing but the larger bones of his mother remained in the meadow.

That had been five seasons ago. Now he ran from no animals, not even other boar grizzly.

Twotoes stirred, hungry again, his foreleg bothering him, and began to work his way down the mountainside. The valley below had provided him sustenance—meat—and he would seek it there again.

Three

WITH CLINT AND RAMÓN setting adobe blocks, and Gideon and little Billy mixing and hauling mortar, they had four feet of the barn wall up by late afternoon, when visitors—the first ever other than Indians—caused them to lay blocks and mortar aside.

Clint heard them coming before he saw them. Hounds brayed, running bush rabbits into the underbrush, while three mounted men plodded along behind on three rough-looking slab-sided mustangs. Two of them led equally sorry-looking pack horses. Each carried a .50 caliber Hawken rifle resting easily across the saddle and each, Clint noted, had an Arkansas toothpick shoved into his belt—a double-edged weapon more for fighting than camp use.

Clint walked to a trough and washed up as they neared. They reined up forty paces away and the leader yelled out, "Hello the house! We got fresh meat if'n ya'll got fire and coffee!"

"Ride on in and make yourself at home," Clint called back.

All three of the men were bearded, buckskinned, and moccasined, with rumpled manes of hair, and smelled of bear grease. The leader looped a leg over the saddle and the horse's withers, then dropped silently to the ground, his ease of movement belying his barrel chest and great size. The buckskins strained at his thick thighs and biceps. The Hawken hung loosely in his large left hand.

He nodded to Clint. "I be Ezekiel Stokes, and these is my

brothers, Mordecai and Obededom. Friends call us Zeke, Mort, and Obe." His eyes narrowed. "You fellas *are* of a mind to be friendly?" Zeke kept a flinty gaze, with eyes the color of topaz, unblinking, on Clint until he stepped forward and extended his hand. Zeke took it in a callused bear-sized paw and they shook.

"That's Ramón Diego on the wall, Gideon LaMont standing below, and the little fellow is Billy Jessup. I'm Clint Ryan and this is my spread." As he talked, Billy ran over and stood slightly behind him.

"As I said," Zeke repeated, "we got meat if'n you got coffee."

"Climb down." Clint motioned to the other two.

The one called Mort, tall and slender with razor features and a high-crowned hat, kept his eyes on the barn where Gideon and Ramón worked, and stayed in the saddle. Finally, he cut his gaze to Obe, who also remained in his saddle. "You don't 'spect a body to be breaking bread with no Ethiopian and no greaser?"

The dogs, big redbone beasts, most of them viciously scarred from encounters with bear and cougar—and each other—milled around the yard sticking their noses into every nook and cranny and occasionally letting out a yapping bark as they did so.

"I don't 'spect they eat in the house with Mr. Ryan here," Zeke said, and moved to the pack horses he led.

"They do!" Clint said quickly, his voice gaining an edge. "They share the house, the food, and anything else on this spread."

Silence descended a moment before the big man's gravelly voice echoed again. "Then we won't be a'stayin' to sup with ya'll." Zeke returned to his mount, but stood beside it, his tone remaining casual. Neither of his brothers had dismounted. "We been huntin' the hills yonder," he offered, trying to lighten the mood.

"Deer and elk?" Clint asked.

"And griz."

"Seen any grizzly?" Clint asked, still trying to be cordial.

"Shot a few last trip. Shot one this time, but he was the toughest critter I ever saw. Ran off with a belly fulla lead and we lost his track."

"Not a two-toed boar, I don't imagine?" Clint pressed.

"Sure was. Lost three toes in one of my snappers. Jerked 'em off like a lizard does 'is tail. . . . Ya'll had trouble with him?"

"Not us, the Indians up north. Wounded bear is a blight on the land," Clint said, his manner hardening.

"Killin' is our business, Ryan. Sometimes they gets away, most often not."

Clint gave him a hard look, saying nothing more and hoping they would ride off. The whole time they had talked, the other two brothers were surveying the surroundings, coveting what they saw, in Clint's estimation.

Ramón finished laying the course of blocks he worked on, then jumped down from the wall. Never far from him was his reata, which he picked up off a pile of adobe blocks and looped over his shoulder. He and Gideon started over—but Gideon paused, then suddenly turned and walked straight for the house.

"We would be obliged if you would trade a hind quarter of our venison for a sack of yer coffee."

"Sounds like a poor trade to me, friend," Clint said, his voice suddenly cold. "I can knock down a deer within a hundred yards of the house. It's two hundred miles to coffee, and we didn't stock up figuring on visitors."

Gideon had disappeared inside the house, but Ramón walked up beside Clint, a smile on his face. Clint raised a foot up onto a stump where Ramón had fastened an anvil, propping an elbow on his knee. He patiently hoped these men would go on about their business, and hoped their business was far from Rancho Kaweah.

"We got a little silver money," Zeke said, still grudgingly hopeful.

"Money's not much good out here, Mr. Stokes," Clint said. "Like fetching coffee, it's two hundred miles to a place to spend it." Ramón began to pick up the hard tone in Clint's voice—and his smile faded. Casually, he let the reata fall from his shoulder and began forming a loop, then recoiling it, then repeating the motion as if it was a habit.

Zeke's look hardened to granite, his glance going from brother to brother before returning to Clint. He fingered his Hawken.

"Maybe we'll trade you some lead for a sack of coffee, and everything else you got in this outhouse you call a spread."

Clint was not one to be threatened.

Before Zeke could raise the barrel of the rifle, Clint drove off the leg he had placed up on the stump, and with a powerful flying lunge, knocked a surprised Zeke Stokes sprawling to the hard ground. Clint landed on top of the big man, the rifle between them—both of them clinging to it.

They rolled across the dust, each fighting for position. Zeke, the larger of the two, managed to get his legs under him and struggled to his feet, dragging Clint up with him. When he was almost face to face with Clint, he flashed an evil grin.

"Ya'll made a bad mistake, takin' on this wolverine!"

"Skunk is more like it," Clint said, but with powerful arms and thick shoulders, Zeke almost drove him back to the ground as he tried to lurch the rifle away.

The other Stokes brothers watched with interest, neither raising a weapon, both smiling and confident in the outcome of this scuffle.

And Zeke did move Clint about with ease, until he drew the more slender man too close, and Clint drove a knee up into Stokes' crotch.

Zeke's broad face went gray-green, and his grip on the Hawken loosened. Clint tried to jerk it away, but Stokes, his face now a mask of pain, managed to hold fast. Clint drove into him, and the big man reacted by shoving forward. Quick as a cat, Clint reversed his force and sat back, getting his feet in Zeke's gut, both of them clinging to the rifle. He rolled and kicked the man in a clumsy flip over him. Zeke landed hard on his back, expelling air in a great "oomph" that echoed over the yard, and released his grip on the rifle.

Clint straddled him, the rifle barrel across the man's thick neck, pinning him to the ground, before he could catch his breath.

Surprised, both Obe and Mort went for their rifles, but Ramón's fast loop caught the fat Obe in the motion, and jerked him from the saddle to the ground, knocking the wind from him with a hollow sound that shamed that which had come from his larger brother.

Mort's rifle hammer ratcheted back, and he snarled, "You're a dead greaser."

Before Ramón could respond, Gideon's voice rang out from the window of the ranch house. "All you'll get for lead is lead . . . and a lotta grief, friend."

They all turned and stared at Gideon at the window. The Colt's revolving breech rifle in his hands was centered on Mort's chest. Mort fingered his weapon nervously, trying to decide if he could get a shot off at the man who was mostly shielded by the window, then eased it to hang casually at his side. Ramón eased the tension on the reata, allowing Obe to shake it off and climb to his feet, now that Gideon had the drop on them.

"No reason this should come to shootin'," Mort said in a low voice.

"Drop that cannon," Gideon commanded, and Mort let his weapon slide carefully to the ground.

"That's a ten-shot Colt's he has there," Clint cautioned, easing his crushing hold on Zeke's throat. The big man coughed and hacked as Clint climbed to his feet and continued speaking. "You fellas better ride on out of here, and don't look back . . . or that 'Ethiopian' will be pissin' on three fresh graves come sunset."

Zeke seemed to consider this a moment as he, too, climbed to his feet, rubbing his reddened throat. He choked again, then spat a long stream of tobacco juice into the dust and backhanded its remnants from his chin. "Let's ride, boys," he said, and swung up on his rough horse with surprising ease. He hesitated before reining away. "Not sharin' a little coffee is downright unneighborly of ya'll."

"You coulda shared a pot at the table with Gideon, Ramón, Billy, and me, mister. It was your choice."

"We'll do without," the big man said. "I'll tell you somethin', pilgrim, we don't take kindly to being drawed down on by no nigger, and I can whip you faster than corn goes through a goose . . . an' I will next time we meet, sure as the sun comes up in the mornin'." Then he reined his horse violently around and spurred him so hard he drew blood from skin drawn taut over ribs. "You ain't seen the last of the Stokes brothers, pilgrim," Zeke yelled out without looking back.

"For your sakes, I hope we have," Clint said quietly.

They rode out in a cloud of dust, dragging their pack horses behind them. Their dogs formed up and chased them out, but before they were out of sight had begun to lead, and soon the sound of their baying was the only reminder of the Stokes brothers.

"What was that all about?" Ramón asked.

"They wanted to make a bad trade" was all Clint said. He started back to the barn, Billy close behind.

"Who were those fellows?" Billy asked excitedly.

"Meat hunters, I imagine," Clint said. "The gold fields have created a great demand for meat, and these fellas were bound to push south when game got scarce up north." His brows furrowed. "They kill everything in sight." Then Clint smiled and ruffled Billy's hair. "Don't worry about them, Billy me lad. There're long gone and it's good riddance."

"Young William!" Gideon shouted from where he had exited the house and started across the yard, still carrying the Colt's. Billy stopped and waited for him to catch up. "I stoked up the fire so you can warm up those pots your pa left. Don't you be burning the grub or I'll chuck you in the river."

Billy ran for the house, tired of hauling mortar anyway. "Let's eat first, then you can chuck me in the river all you want."

Clint smiled at the two, but his mind remained on the Stokes brothers. He had a real bad feeling about the last two days. First he had turned down his neighbors from the south, the Tule Yocuts, then he had been forced to refuse to share even a little coffee with his first white visitors, and even choke one of them half to death and run them all off at gunpoint. Hell, it was not the best start for a new home. He hoped it was not an unlucky one.

Then again, maybe the Stokes boys would kill the bear with the missing toes that had been bothering the Yocuts.

Hell, he'd share a little coffee with *even them* if they'd handle the job he'd shirked—and take the threat from the Tule River tribe. He shrugged it off and went back to the adobe wall.

"Those three'll bear watching," Gideon said quietly.

"Just keep ol' Colt's close by. . . . Thank God there's only three of them." Clint stopped in his tracks, a big adobe block in his hands. "What made you head for the rifle like that, Gideon?"

"You learn to read a man when you're a slave. That's stayed with me even as a freedman. The way he stands, the glint in his eye, and how you act or don't act may mean you get the lash . . . or worse." Gideon shook his head sagely. "I could tell from forty paces that ol' man Stokes had evil on his mind."

"Well," Clint pondered, "for whatever reason, it's a damn good thing you did. That pudgy one on the roan's got about as much good sense as a box of rocks. The only thing worse than a mean man is a mean ignorant one. And the other one had about as mean a look as I've ever seen. From now on, we'll keep a weapon in the barn and one in the smokehouse."

As he returned to work, Clint noticed a low sound, concentrated on it, and realized it was a quiet whining. He searched the yard with his gaze, but could not find the source. Had one of the dogs stayed behind? He walked toward the house and rounded the corner. Floppy-eared, red as a bay horse, the hound lay under some buckbrush a few feet from the house. At Clint's approach, the dog inched forward on his belly, his head canting from one side to the other, his tail wagging.

Clint knelt down beside him. The animal carried a wicked gash in his side, festered and putrid.

Billy ran up behind Clint and leaned down with his hands on his knees. "Gol'darn! They left one of their dogs."

"This ol' fellow stayed of his own accord because he was having trouble keeping up . . . and I don't want to hear you swearing!" Billy glanced up guiltily. "Fetch him some scraps from the smokehouse, Billy boy." The boy hurried away and Clint rose, rounded the house, and yelled to Ramón.

"Hey, *amigo,* we need some doctoring over here."

The slender vaquero hurried away from his job at the wall and joined him. "What happened?" he asked, worried that something was wrong with Clint or Billy.

"The Stokes boys left us a boarder. But a sick one."

Within moments, they were holding the redbone hound while Ramón cleaned the wound. The dog didn't like it, but he didn't complain much considering how it must have pained him. He seemed to sense they were helping him. He ate a little and drank some water Billy brought him, then crawled back under the buckbrush and fell quickly asleep as the men returned to their job.

As Billy carried mortar, he kept up a barrage of questions, directed at whoever was closest.

"Can we name him?"

"You name him, Billy."

"Whose dog will he be?"

"He's the Stokeses', at least until we know they've left him for good."

"Then whose will he be?"

"Why don't we let him decide, if it comes to that? He'll probably favor whoever feeds him and takes good care of him . . . and that includes keeping his mess outta the yard here." That brought a wink between the men.

"Is he gonna get well?"

"The good Lord is the only one who knows that," Clint answered.

And on and on, until even Ramón had tired of his questions when Billy started repeating himself the third time.

"Young Guillermo, go and check your pots," Ramón suggested. "Before someone mistakes you for a magpie and takes a slingshot to you."

"Yes, sir," Billy said. He ran for the house.

"Do you think they'll be back for the dog?" Gideon asked as they began to clean up and gather their tools.

"They had more than a dozen hounds," Clint answered. "I doubt if they'll miss this one." He secretly hoped they wouldn't. A dog, he suddenly realized, would add to the rancho. And Billy needed a friend.

By the time Zeke, Mort, and Obe rode back into their camp, the sun was below the horizon. They had set up their base camp in a wide meadow along the main branch of the Kaweah River, not far below where the much smaller South Fork joined it, where the oak-and-digger-pine-covered foothills were beginning to get serious about becoming mountains. In the distance, where no white men had ever been, rose a great granite half-dome.

Six other buckskinned men worked about the camp. Two Swedes, Johanson and Petersen; three Missourians, Haskins, Polkinghorn, and Brandt; and O'Rourke, an Irishman. All of the men were skilled in the outdoors. Two heavy wagons rested in hulking canvas-covered silence flanking the campfire. Iron snap-traps of a variety of sizes hung from their planked sides. Two dozen hogshead barrels—some full of salt, some of salted meat, some empty—sat or lay on their sides in disarray about the camp, and a half-dozen carcasses hung from the limbs of the short oaks beyond. A table of split logs held a deer carcass being butchered by a blood-soaked man in a floppy hat. Skins of deer, bear, and antelope lay everywhere, in various stages of tanning, some stretched on hoops of river willow. Pits full of mashed brains, ash, and water, a terrible gruel used for tanning, were dug around the perimeter of the camp and a few held soaking hides. Flies and mosquitoes and gnats buzzed in cloudy profusion, pestering men and animals, the sound of them occluding even the sound of the nearby river, which bounded and leapt rocks in joyous disdain of the grisly scene so close to its banks.

The stench of death permeated everything, and the men worked and ate and lived their lives with it hanging over them—the smell alone created a solemnity about the place.

As soon as they arrived, the dogs began circling the outside of the camp, seeking the fat scraped from the hides or the bones thrown carelessly to the camp's perimeter. The dogs knew from past experience not to enter the camp itself, for to do so meant being on the receiving end of a hot firebrand pulled from the fire and flung with hair-scorching accuracy.

"Did you get the coffee?" Sam Polkinghorn, a burly, red-headed, red-bearded man, asked, wiping his bloody hands on his buckskins as the three brothers reined up.

"Som'bitch had coffee, but he's a'keepin' it," Zeke snarled and dismounted. His anger had grown since being forced to ride away from the ranch.

"That's a hell of a note. Did ya'll offer to knot his head?"

Zeke gave him a hard look, then cut his eyes to his brothers with an unsaid warning that he would whip them both if they said a word about his getting knocked down and damn near choked to death. He centered his hard gaze back on Polkinghorn. "He'll pay for slightin' a Stokes," Zeke growled, "sure as Tennessee men is rawhide tough an' wolverine"—he again gave his brothers a warning glance—"wolverine mean."

The other men in the camp gathered around, and the word of no coffee spread among them. They grumbled and groused, for they had been more than a week without.

"What's for supper?" Mort asked as he too dropped from the saddle.

"Boiled venison," Polkinghorn said.

"That's good," Mort said sarcastically, taking off the high-crowned hat and sailing it to a nearby rock. "We had it for the last two weeks, why not again?"

"Anytime you want to cook, I'll be happy to go gallivantin' around the country with yer brothers," Polkinghorn said, and his face reddened to match his beard. "If ya'll had brought the coffee, it'd be easier to wash the goat down."

"Both of ya shudup," Zeke snapped. "The faster we'n fill these hogsheads, the faster we'll be back to the gold fields fillin' our pockets with the dust those fools been grubbin' outta the mud. They'll pay three dollar a pound for this salted deer an' antelope meat, and more for the bear. Then ya'll can have a bath in coffee if'n ya'll's inclined to baths."

"A cup would do me fine. A right camp would have coffee,"

Polkinghorn grumbled, turning back to his fire and pot of boiling venison. "This ain't no kinda layout to work for. . . ."

Zeke smashed the butt of the Hawken into the side of Polkinghorn's head, splattering blood onto the rock ring of the fire. The cook went down in a heap, his shoulder just touching the edge of the campfire. The smell of burning buckskin began to fill the camp, overwhelming that of rotting meat.

The men moved forward to see the result of Zeke's anger, and Obe, still sitting his horse, crept the muzzle of his Hawken up until it quietly threatened the men. "I can shoot one of 'em for ya, Zeke. I can, don't ya know!"

Zeke took a threatening step toward the gathering men. "You boys do what I say, when I say, and don't go a'flappin' your jaws at me. We'd a'brought the coffee but that pilgrim down where the smoke come from was real niggardly. We shoulda knowed . . . a white man what took up with a greaser and a no-account Ethiopian. We'll get around to him an' his mangy crew afore we head outta here."

One of the men reached down and dragged Sam Polkinghorn away from the fire, as his matted beard had begun to smoke and the stench of burning hair joined that of buckskin.

"Leave him lay," Zeke growled, leaning forward. "Serves him right, and any man who backtalks me'll get the same . . . or worse."

The man immediately dropped Sam and retreated.

"Someone finish that mess he was a'cookin', and throw some greens in it if you lazy louts can locate 'em afore it be too dark to find any."

Zeke led his horse away to where another dozen horses and mules were staked out. Beyond them, a dozen oxen grazed in the failing light.

Zeke's brothers joined him, staking out their horses.

"These boys is gettin' a little restless," Mort said. "We best be getting these hogsheads topped off and be headin' back."

"These 'boys' is a'galding my backside," Zeke said. "We sure as hell don't need a half-dozen shirkers to split the take with. Not only will we split the take from the meat, but we'll have five or six dozen head a' fine horseflesh to sell. The two a' you can drive the wagons, I'll push the horses. A four-way split will suit me just fine."

"Four-way?" Obe asked.

"Four-way," Zeke repeated, his eyes narrowing. "One for you, one for Mort, and two for the bossman . . . me. You got a problem with that, little brother?"

"No, Zeke. Does that mean Mort and me'll get more'n we would if'n we split . . . let's see." Obe counted on his fingers. "If'n we split nine ways?"

"That means a lot more for you. More'n two times," Zeke said.

"Sure enuf," Mort said, "more'n two times for you and me, Obe, and more'n four times for big brother Zeke here."

Zeke bent and picked up a round river stone to drive his picket pin into the ground, then he looked at his hawk-faced brother as if he was more than willing to knot his head with the rock. "That's right, Mort. You got any problem with doin' it thataway?"

"Sounds fair to me," Mort muttered, but his tone said different.

"But we ain't got no five-dozen horses," Obe said, scratching his head.

"We will have, after we visit that pilgrim again." Zeke laughed for the first time since he had left camp early that morning.

It was dark, with only the light of the fire to guide them when they walked back to camp. The whole place was strangely silent as they finished off the boiled venison and bedded down.

As always, Zeke lay awake until the breathing of the other men whispered evenly in the silence, broken only by an occasional cough and the night sounds of owl and insect and the continual rippling song of the river. Then he arose from his bedroll, leaving it rumpled as if someone was asleep there, and walked off into the underbrush, carrying his Hawken and eighteen-inch Arkansas toothpick, and bedded down where none of the others knew his location—not even his brothers.

.   .   .   .   .

Twotoes also slept alone.

He awoke feeling better than he had since he had faced the dogs and the men at his high mountain retreat, more than a month ago. Last night, after cresting the long blue granite ridge, he had turned over a log and managed to swat several scampering mice from a nest of mother and almost full-grown babes, in addition to finding a particularly large infestation of termites with three pounds of fat succulent grubs. After that small feast, he slept in a stand of puzzle bark pine, ponderosa, awakening only when the sun warmed his shoulders.

A long narrow valley lay below him. A narrow river worked its way this way and that around flat slabs of granite among white and Douglas fir and dark Jeffrey pine. Twotoes stretched, working the knots out of muscles and the kinks from his joints. He arose on his hind legs and stretched his full length against a three-foot-diameter ponderosa pine, marking it as high as he could reach with his long foreclaws, nearly eleven feet. Then he spun and, feeling good in the caress of the morning sun, loped down the slope in front of him. With longer hind than fore legs, he was clumsy trying to travel downhill—and had to slow several times to keep from tumbling end over end—but the river below was inviting, and he knew that in the shallow pools between low waterfalls he would find succulent fish.

He stopped to bat around a pile of sugar pine cones, their foot-long shapes too interesting to resist, then continued until he reached the river bank. Edging himself out on a long low granite slab, he poised over a pool and remained as still as the granite boulders flanking the river, watching, waiting, enjoying the warmth of the morning sun on his broad back and shoulders. He was gaining weight, returning strength to his wide shoulders and back and tree-trunk-thick hind legs. Without the gnawing hunger in his stomach and pain deep in his gut, he had the patience to sit still as a stone, with only his small eyes moving, and wait for an unwary trout to venture too close to his lightning-fast paw.

He waited in stony silence.

High on a ridge overlooking the south fork of the Kaweah,

where they had been tracking a buck deer whose deep dewclaw marks testified to his size, Obe and Mort Stokes crouched in the shade of a buckeye and studied the dark spot on the river's edge far below.

"Can you make out if'n it is or if'n it ain't?" Obe asked.

"Looks like it might be just a bush a'growin' there," Mort said, studying the shape far below.

Suddenly, the bush jumped into the water.

"Hell no!" Mort said, lowering his voice. "That's a by-God griz, sure as I'm Tennessee tough."

"And us without the dogs," Obe said unhappily.

"It's three mile or more back to camp. We can fetch a couple a' more men and the hounds and still run the fool a few mile before sundown. Could be he'll turn on the dogs like the fightin' fiend they are and we'll a'catch 'im afore sundown."

"What about this here buck we're trackin'?"

"Obe, you're dumb as a stick. That bear'll go over six hun'erd pounds an' dress out at over four. That's over a thousand dollars. Now get to puttin' one foot in front of the other."

In twenty minutes of hard downhill walking, the two hunters were back at the camp saddling their horses and collecting the hounds. Zeke had decided he would lead the hunt, and they would take Polkinghorn with them—he might cause trouble if left. He had awakened with a terrible headache, and stayed real quiet all morning long. Zeke decided he wanted the man where he could keep an eye on him. Besides, a good ten-mile ride and probably a few miles afoot in the mountains, carrying a nine-pound Hawken and a pack of grub and blanket, had a tendency to take the fight out of the best of men. Particularly after coming face to face with six to seven hundred pounds of teeth, claws, and pure old devil mean.

A dozen dogs set out with the four mounted men. They would be yipping and sniffing along until they got near the place Obe and Mort had spotted the big silvertip and picked up his spoor. Then it would be Katy-bar-the-door as they took up the baying as old as time itself.

They would run the griz until he turned to fight—and a dozen redbone hounds and four Hawken .50 calibers would be too much for even six or seven hundred pounds of pure hell.

By nightfall, with luck, ol' griz would be four hundred pounds of salted meat and a fine bear rug.

Four

THE ADOBE PORTION of the small thirty-by-fifty-foot barn was finished with oak headers over its four windows and its front and back wide double doors by the time they finished work on Sunday night. Now the rancho almost had three buildings. All that was left was the second floor of logs, raftering, roofing, and hanging the doors and shuttering the windows, but that was easier said than done. It was miles to where the tall straight pine began—lodgepole or Jeffrey—and they would have to be cut and hauled, or floated down the Kaweah, which the men had decided was worth a try—and they would try to find a cedar to float, which they would split for shingles.

Billy had named the dog Smiley, and the men had to agree that the animal did have a propensity to curl its lips in a foolish dog grin when approached. The choice had been between Smiley and Wags, for obvious reasons, and Smiley had won out, as Wags seemed a bit condescending to a full-grown bear-tracking redbone hunting hound. The dog had joined them at the barn all Sunday long, and the gash in his side had scabbed over cleanly after Ramón scrubbed and treated the wound with wild rosemary.

Even with his joy over Smiley, Billy had grown more and more quiet as Sunday wore on, missing his father, Gordy, who stayed absent from the rancho.

As they washed up for supper in the growing darkness, Clint finally addressed the subject.

"Your dad must have found some color in one of those foothill streams, Billy."

"He shoulda been back by now," the boy said, scrubbing his hands in the trough.

"He'll be along. I wouldn't worry about him even if he doesn't show up by bedtime. He's gettin' to be a real hand. He'll be fine."

Billy looked up, but his look said he knew Clint was just being nice—Gordy was no hand in the wilds, even though he was trying hard to become one. Not trying to become a rancher, or drover, but a prospector. What Billy did not know was that Clint had discovered more than ten pounds of flour and a side of bacon missing. They had a small hogshead of beans, so he could not tell if five or ten pounds of those were gone—but he suspected they were, as well as some salt and sugar and coffee. It looked to Clint like Gordy meant to be gone a hell of a lot longer than the twenty-four hours he had claimed.

Since it was Sunday and since Gordy was not there to tend the stove, Ramón had pulled one of the sandhill cranes from the smokehouse where it had hung a few days, then slow-roasted it, spitted over an outside low-ember fire on a green willow branch, all afternoon. The ten-pound bird had taken on a golden brown, basting in its own juices as one or the other of the four took turns at the makeshift spit, turning it slowly and seasoning it with salt and hot pork fat, then collecting the drippings in a bucket. They had also buried a generous portion of plump tule roots, wrapped in a blanket of wild grape leaves, and covered the nutty-tasting tubers with coals. Ramón collected some of the bird drippings and fetched them to the stove inside and made a fine gravy by adding a little flour and water. That and the usual corn mush and beans graced the table, as well as golden brown drop biscuits. Ramón had also made a pie from the last of the dried apples they had.

They sat down to a feast.

As Clint sipped his coffee after the meal, he felt a twinge of regret at not giving the hunters, the Stokes brothers, a sack of the brown beans they had sought. He had made a snap judgment about the men, and had not acted exactly neighborly. Hell, neighbors were hard to come by, in fact, nonexistent, on the Kaweah—except for the Yocuts. Even if the Stokes brothers were dead set against blacks and Mexicans, and probably against Indians as well, they could learn, as Clint had, not to judge a man by anything other than how he did his work and what kind of friend he was.

But Clint had had the advantage of working for a dozen years of his life on shipboard, where men from all over the world joined together on merchant vessels—and where, when your life was in another man's hands, it mattered little what his color or language was. All that mattered was that he did his job, and cared about the man next to him on the yardarm. And Clint had been alone and looking for friends. The Stokes brothers had each other to depend on. Clint had found that groups of men were much less receptive to new ideas—they had each other to agree with, even if their premise was just plain wrong in the eyes of other men and most likely in the all-seeing eyes of God.

Gideon expected prejudice, not that he would back away from any man, but he would shrug it off so long as a man did not come between him and what needed doing.

Ramón, the proud vaquero, was another matter altogether. If he had overheard Zeke Stokes' remark, Zeke might have found himself wrapped in Ramón's reata and slung from the nearest oak. At least Ramón would have given it a whirl.

Gideon, on the other hand, would keep his hands to himself until it came to fighting time, and fighting time for the ex-slave was only when there was no other choice—and then he fought to end it, no matter what it took. Other choices did not include backing down, only avoiding what did not absolutely have to be. Gideon could be a real diplomat—he even spoke French and sounded like one on occasion—or he could be a devil with guns or fists or blade.

Clint walked out to the big corral, actually forty acres of fenced spring-fed meadow, the first job he and Gideon had undertaken when they had arrived on the Kaweah after driving the horses from the Vegas' place, Rancho del Río Ancho, on the Sacramento. They had built a smaller remuda corral for the riding stock, and an even smaller breaking pen of solid walled upright logs. Now the herd had grown to sixty-two with those they had caught in the tules and the addition of eight foals. But only fifty-five animals grazed in the big corral now. They kept six animals in a remuda in the small corral adjacent to the new barn. One of those riding horses was gone, as well as a halter and pack-broke horse from the big corral. Gordy had taken them to the hills.

The cattle grazed free in the tules and low foothills, and the swine ran free in the scrub oak thicket, feeding on the acorns. The sheep were in the high country with a hired Indian shepherd.

With the last of the twilight, while the meadowlarks chirped their final goodbye to the day, Clint leaned on the rail of the main paddock and made a quick count of the Andalusian mares and the mustangs, then walked a ways farther down the rail fence and checked the stallions. Ten of the forty acres were divided into three smaller corrals—fenced a rail higher than the main corral— and the four stallions, separated by an empty corral, resided there.

Two of the big Andalusians had been vying for leader of the big band and had fought almost to the death on two different occasions. Keeping them separated, and each in the company of a less dominant stallion, resolved most of the problems.

Satisfied that all was well with the horses, Clint walked slowly back to the yard. As he neared the house, he heard a quiet sob from around the corner, eased up, and slyly peered around.

Billy, kneeling by Smiley, quietly patted the big redbone hound. He sobbed again, his face in the animal's fur, while Clint watched. Clint backed away from the corner out of sight of Billy, cleared his throat loudly, then strode around the corner.

"Is that you, Billy boy?"

"Yes, sir."

"What are you doing out here in the dark . . . checking on ol' Smiley?"

"Yes, sir."

"Good boy. We need a good hand like you on the place."

Billy said nothing, but kept scratching Smiley's ears. The dog licked his other hand, salty from wiping away the tears.

"Why don't you come inside now. Smiley will keep watch over the place until you get back on the job tomorrow."

Billy arose and sighed deeply. "My pa's still not back. I need to go hunt for him."

"Come on inside. There's a sliver of that apple pie left. If you'd eat it, it would keep Ramón, Gideon, and me from squabbling over it."

"Do you think he'll get back tonight?"

"If he doesn't, there's nothing to worry about. Like I told you today, he probably found a touch of color in one of those creeks. You know how much your daddy wants to find a little gold, so if he did, he won't leave until it's played out . . . and he knows you're in good hands with folks that care about you."

"Then . . . then you won't give him the boot if he's not back on time?"

"Give him the boot? A fine hand like Gordy? Not on your life, Billy me lad. I'd not only lose him, but I'd lose my best hand."

"Best hand?" Billy said.

"You, Billy boy."

Billy laughed. Forgetting his troubles for a moment, he followed Clint inside.

"Ramón," Clint called out to the slender vaquero, who was drying the last of the dinner tins, "how about you and I picking out a high-spirited cayuse for Billy tomorrow, so he can help us on the next horse hunt?"

"Suits me," Ramón said, eyeing the boy. "When I was Billy's size, I had been riding for ten years."

"Since you were only one," Billy said, quickly doing his sums.

"Well, maybe five years," Ramón corrected.

"That's great," Billy said, his grin lighting the room. "My own horse. He will be mine, won't he? Can I help pick?"

"Not unless you get a good night's sleep," Clint said, laughing at the boy's excitement, knowing he probably could not sleep for hours now.

"Young Guillermo," Ramón said, "you crawl between the blankets, then in the morning I'll personally take you to the big corral." Ramón ruffled Billy's hair with a calloused brown hand.

"What's a Guillermo?" Billy asked, badly pronouncing his own name, his brow furrowed as if Ramón had called him something disrespectful.

"That is how William is said in *español* . . . Spanish," Ramón said. His stoic face broke into a smile.

"Oh . . . I guess that's all right." Billy ran for the pole-built rawhide-strung cot that served as his bed, then he slid to a stop before reaching it and turned back.

"How about 'young Guillermo' having that last sliver of pie?" Then he laughed so hard at his newfound name that he brought a grin to the men's faces.

Twotoes had been running for hours.

He had climbed back up to the blue rock ridge, and now rested in a manzanita thicket. The baying of the pack of hounds far in the distance niggled at him and would not allow him respite. He had thought about circling and waiting by the trail for the pack and for the man-animals who followed, but the memory of the pain that had resided so long in his gut was too fresh in his mind. No, he would not lie in wait for them, not unless they got too near. He would run—now that he could run.

And run he did.

Up the river for a few miles, up a gorge the way he had come from the blue ridge while the light of day faded, then finally onto the ridge itself in the semidarkness of a moonlit night. Until the sound of the dogs was lost behind him. Then he lay and rested—but then the sound came again, haunting him. He had not actually seen his pursuers, but he did not have to. He could hear and smell them and had seen their kind before.

Now that he was in the high country, he was more confident. Familiar stands of lodgepole pine and the comforting smell of bear clover—a natural insect repellent—mounds of manzanita-covered granite, towering puzzle bark ponderosa pines with deep-shadowed skunk cabbage and fern-covered meadows winding between great needled giants, all welcomed him from where he lay for miles and miles to the east. They beckoned him, and the baying dogs in the distance encouraged him to move on. He rose and stretched, then the old pain hit him again. He stopped, motionless for a moment, confused by what he could not see and consequently could not fight.

The gut-wrenching pain had not bothered him for more than two days, but the long strenuous climb must have awakened the creatures deep in his insides—only now they'd matured, become fanged snakes.

He must change his strategy. Coughing a deep barking hack, he started down, but away from the sounds pursuing him. He would circle them, back the way he had come, careful to avoid steep slopes, for he could not move quickly down steep grades.

He set out at a lope, his great body rocking steadily back and forth with the rhythmical pounding of his padded feet on the rock and soil, in a clumsy sideways manner that seemed to lessen the hurt inside.

Now they knew it was the two-toed bear they hunted, and it whetted Zeke's appetite even more. He took it personally when an animal outwitted him, and this bear had.

The horses were finished, their hooves torn by the climb up the steep rocky cleft behind the baying hounds, exhausted from the night-long slipping and sliding on steep game trails where sharp shards of rock pierced the soft frogs in the center of hard hooves or cut their hocks. Pointed spears of manzanita pierced their legs and chest and raked their heaving sides. Trembling, fight gone, the exhausted horses stood quietly as Zeke, Mort, Obe, and Sam stripped bridles, saddles, and pack saddles from them.

"Drop them where they fall," Zeke said. Even his voice strained with the exhaustion of the hard night's effort. "These worthless nags'll make their way back to camp; we can pick up the gear later. Pack yer pockets and knapsacks with jerky and biscuits. Every man is on his own with what he can carry, so don't none a' ya be askin' me for grub."

"Can't we rest here awhile?" Obe complained.

"No!" Zeke roared. "I got the feeling he's about to turn on us. Look here," he said, kneeling by the spoor. "His gait is shorter. He stopped here and rested. And he's a big one . . . hind paw 'pears to be fifteen inches. Bigger than even you two blumberheads thought." Zeke picked up his small canvas knapsack in one hand and his Hawken in the other and set out. "This'n'll go seven hund'erd easy . . . maybe eight. We're a'gonna get him afore the sun rolls across the noon sky."

He slapped the mustang that had carried him so far, so nobly, on the rump and started him back down the narrow game trail. "Get on, ya lazy knothead," Zeke groused. The other horses fell in behind, stumbling and limping.

Far out ahead of them, the dogs bayed on, seemingly unaffected by the long night's struggle. The echo of the age-old chase seemed as strong as it had in the valley far below, at its beginning over twelve hours earlier.

Zeke strode out ahead, climbing a steep narrow cleft in the rocks that had convinced him it was time to abandon the horses. Mort followed close behind. Farther back, Obe struggled to work his way up between the rocks.

Sam stood, his hands on his hips, watching the men climb, trying to decide if he was, in fact, going to follow, or turn and pursue the horses back to the camp far below. His head throbbed as if a tiny blacksmith worked with a red-hot forge deep inside it, and he feared his cheekbone was broken from the whack he had taken from that big dumb brute, Zeke Stokes. Every once in a while, his head would swim and he felt as if he might pass out, or worse, puke in front of the men.

"Any man," Zeke's gravel voice rang out, "who shirks or turns tail is gonna get an ounce of lead from Mr. Hawken's finest right up his cowardly arse."

Sam Polkinghorn looked up to the crown of the rock ridge thirty paces above. Zeke stood, sparks in his eyes, shaking his Hawken at him. Sam put his head down, got his courage up, and started to climb.

"I was just a'waitin' till Obe got outta the way," he grumbled, but thought, *and until I can get a shot at yer fat back, you greasy Tennessee roothog.* He had thought about backshooting Zeke a dozen times since they had taken up the chase, and would have, except he knew Mort, or even that dunderheaded Obe, would get a shot off at him before he could reload. No, he would hang in there, fight the pain and dizziness for one reason—to kill the big ugly som'bitch who had clubbed him down like a cur in front of his friends.

He climbed, holding his knapsack in one hand and his Hawken in the other, slipping and sliding, scraping knees and knuckles, until he crested the top. Zeke, Mort, and Obe moved out ahead— Zeke an easy forty-pace shot in front, his back an inviting target.

Sam looked back down the cleft, wondering if he could get off a quick shot and then slide down the narrow ravine and escape.

No, it was too risky. He would bide his time.

It would come. Good things always came to those who waited.

Billy stuffed his breakfast in so fast he did not even pause to ask why his father had not shown up in the night. The instant he had cleaned his plate of beans, bacon, and biscuits, he carried his tin to the bucket of water that sat on the plank counter, and scraped, washed, and dried it and his spoon, then turned to Ramón.

"You 'bout finished?"

"What is your hurry, young Guillermo?" Ramón said, and winked at Gideon and Clint.

"You didn't forget about the . . . the cayuse, did you?"

"Cayuse?" Ramón teased.

"You said you were going to pick me out one this morning."

"And pick you out one I will . . . as soon as I finish this plate and this cup of coffee."

"I'll wait outside," Billy said, and ran to see how Smiley had fared the night.

Ramón turned to Clint. "I seem to remember his father denying him a horse."

"He didn't have one to give," Clint said. "I do."

"Well, then I am going to teach him right. He will break his own, and make the saddle and bridle with his own hands before he earns the right to ride."

"I never expected anything else," Clint said. He was not about to get in the way of what Ramón was the best in the world at. "I don't know how Billy will take to that, but I never expected less."

"He will take to it just fine," Ramón said. "If he wants to ride."

As Ramón got up and hauled his tin and spoon to the bucket of water, Gideon looked up from his plate. "You two are about as much fun as getting hung with a new rope. I'll do these pots and skillet up while you go out and torture that young'un."

Clint and Ramón gave Gideon a "harrumph" and headed for the door, Clint pulling his flat-brimmed tan hat over his sandy hair as Ramón fitted a flat-brimmed black hat over equally black hair. Passing the peg where it hung, the vaquero slid his reata over his shoulder.

Outside, Billy and Smiley waited. The dog matched Billy's grin, trotting along behind the men, who strode out toward the big corral.

They leaned on the top rail and studied the herd of Andalusians and mustangs.

"How old is that little paint mare?" Clint asked, referring to one of the mustangs.

"Too young. Do you want the boy to have one of the bush horses or one of the blooded stock?"

Clint pondered this a moment. "Thirteen or fourteen hands is enough horse for the boy. Pick out a nice little mare."

Ramón curled a lip at him, as Clint expected he would. "A mare is no animal for a man . . . even a boy, to ride. I will find a small stallion with a natural quietness about him. The boy can handle fourteen and a half, maybe even fifteen hands."

"I can, Mr. Ryan," Billy assured him as he climbed up to the top rail to sit. Smiley seemed unhappy that he could not join them atop the rail, but finally he propped his forefeet up on the third rail and looked through, happily panting.

"Do you see the little palomino?" Ramón asked, pointing.

"Just like your horse, Mr. Ryan. Just like Diablo."

"He's a lot of animal," Clint cautioned.

"He is four or more years, and calm, and he will train," Ramón said with confidence.

"What do you think, Billy me lad?" Clint asked, already knowing the answer.

"He's beautiful," Billy said, beaming.

"Then the palomino it is," Clint said.

Ramón slid off the rail and made his way to the horses, who looked up expectantly at his approach. He clucked with his tongue, and got them bunched, working them back to a corner of the corral. Making a wide loop, he began a slow twirl and edged closer to the small herd of horses, some of which broke to his right and some to the left. Suddenly, the circling loop quickened, then sailed into the group on the left.

As the rest of the horses fled, hooves pounding hollowly in the meadow grass, the little palomino was left alone, facing the interloper. His forelegs stiffened against the pull of the reata, his nostrils flared, and the whites of his wide eyes showed around the big brown corneas.

"He got him!" Billy said wonderingly.

"Don't spook him," Clint cautioned in a low tone. Almost all the horses had been trained to the halter, and some of them even wore headstalls, signifying that they would lead, and many of those could be packed. But if they had been broken to the saddle, fully trained, they would have resided in the remuda corral.

The palomino wore no headstall, and had probably seen only a few minutes at the end of a reata, much less a lead rope.

He sat back against the pull of Ramón's sixty-five-foot woven rawhide. Ramón coiled the reata as he quietly approached the stud, then sat back quickly, a hand behind his back holding the loops of the line and another stretched out, jerking down as the stallion reared on his hind legs, lashing out with his forefeet.

Billy's eyes widened.

"He's pretty wild!" the boy said.

"They all are to begin with," Clint said reassuringly. "You'll be riding him in no time. After you spend a few weeks breaking him and he comes to love you."

"Couldn't we get one already broken?"

"You said you wanted that one," Clint said, furrowing his brows at the boy in feigned disappointment.

"I do, I do," Billy said quickly. "He's great."

"Then get ready for a few weeks' hard work, Billy boy. Ramón won't like it if you shirk and complain, and he'll be a lot more likely to give up on you than on the palomino. If you want to ride, you have to learn from the beginning, and there's no better way to do it than learning *with* the horse."

"We're going to learn together?"

"Together. While you make a saddle and bridle to ride with. You're going to have plenty to do, Billy boy . . . and, my young friend, that's all in addition to your other chores."

"Yes, sir."

The horse did seem to be calm for an unbroken animal, but still he continued to set back against the lead rope. Ramón shook the loop loose and flipped it over the animal's head, releasing him, then walked, with Billy and Smiley following closely, to the remuda to saddle his own gray stallion. He returned to the big corral astride, and roped the little palomino again, this time by the forelegs, jerking him off his feet. Ramón dismounted while his gray backed, keeping the palomino off his feet. With a rawhide pigging string, Ramón hogtied the palomino and removed the reata. He put a *jáquima*, or hackamore, on the animal, took another lead rope and tied it to the palomino's light blond tail and to the headstall, pulling the animal's head around tightly as he did so, then released the horse's legs. The horse stumbled to his feet, tied head to tail so all he could do was move in a circle.

"Aren't you gonna hurt him?" Billy called out with a worried tone. He gained only a disdainful glance from Ramón, as the palomino stood confused. Ramón snapped the pigging string at the little horse, who jumped in fear, but found himself only circling when he tried to run away. Each time he quieted, Ramón again snapped the string and caused him to move until the animal stood in utter exhaustion. Ramón left him panting, and walked to where Billy sat on the fence.

"You must make him understand that it is fruitless to pull against the line on his neck. When he is sufficiently spent, we will make him understand that the rope is his friend."

"You won't hurt him," Billy said again, fearing Ramón's hard look but fearing him hurting the animal even more.

"He will not hurt himself," Ramón corrected. "I will only use his own strength against him. You and I, young William, are not strong enough to train this fine animal if we had to use only the feeble muscle God gave man. We must use the *cabeza,* the head. He must be made to use his own strength against himself. Would you hurt yourself?"

"No," Billy said sheepishly, beginning to understand.

After another session tying the horse so he would spin the other way, the animal stood in complete exhaustion, lathered from fighting his own reluctance to stand calm. He stood quietly while the vaquero replaced the reata around his neck—and he no longer set his legs when the man attempted to lead him, but followed.

The vaquero tied him to the top rail near where Billy sat and doubled the pigging string and placed it over the horse's neck. Ramón began to pull the string back and forth, like a man shining his boots, moving the string up and down from withers to head. At first the animal flared his eyes in fear, then he settled, and at last twitched his nose and nickered quietly, seeming to enjoy it.

"This is called *quitando las coquillas* . . . let's see, you would say . . . removing the ticklishness," Ramón said, then looked over his shoulder and smiled at Billy for the first time since the process had begun. He seemed pleased with the horse's progress.

Ramón had the animal well calmed and convinced he could do nothing but follow the lead of the reata, and started for the gate while Clint slid its four rails aside.

Billy, Smiley close at his side, followed a few cautious steps behind the horse as Clint fell into step with Ramón.

"Billy's wondering if maybe he shouldn't have been happy with shank's mare," Clint commented.

"He will wonder a lot more before he sits this little *caballo* the first time."

"He'll be better for it," Clint said confidently.

"They both will," Ramón echoed.

Five

AFTER AN HOUR of daydreaming about what he would do with his money, Gordy Jessup rose from the flat rock he sat upon, spread his arms wide, and yelled with pure joy as he did a little jig, his exuberant cries echoing up and down the narrow canyon.

A pile of boulders choked the narrow ravine, its sides almost vertical, its bottom a five-foot-wide bubbling creek. Gordy had come to this spot by entering a wide-mouthed canyon lined with sycamores. At one spot a twenty-foot waterfall faced him, but relentless, he studied the rock escarpment until he found a narrow game trail, and led the horses, slipping and sliding, up, up, until he could mount again. The boulder-strewn canyon floor narrowed and the walls of the canyon got steeper until the golden-cup live oaks that billowed from the sides almost touched. Then the river willows began thickening along the creek sides until they grew to the canyon rock walls, and he was forced to unsaddle and stake the horses out in a patch of needlegrass where they could both graze and reach the creek, and walk on in the bottom of the flow itself. Every once in a while he could see rock ledges protruding from the dark green on the steep walls overhead. Not just common granite ledges, but granite laced with great ribs of white quartz— and he had studied enough to know that quartz sometimes played host to the precious yellow metal.

Finally, the willows formed a complete canopy overhead. It was not unpleasant in the tunnel of green. In fact, even with the sun climbing in the morning sky, it was cool there.

Fingerling trout and a few pan-size ones scattered ahead of him in the occasional pools of shaded water when he stepped from rock to rock, until he finally gave up the clumsy brook toe-dance and just slopped ahead, letting his brogans get soaked through.

Every once in a while, he would pause and pan a little, kneeling by the bubbling creek, studying the lay of its boulder-strewn gravel bottom, grubbing out a handful of sand and pebbles with his hands. He had gotten no color, but he was not discouraged. This was a gold-looking spot if he had ever seen one. Eventually, the creek bed widened a bit, and he faced a wall of boulders where a slide had filled the narrow cleft—but it did not stop the creek. Demanding waters, incessant in their push for the valley bottom, worked their way through the toe of the twenty-foot-high impediment. A thousand tiny rivulets of water pushed through crack and cranny to join up again as one. And the rocks and boulders had not only relinquished the space between them, but had given their surface to moss; above, higher on the dam, gold and green and yellow lichen fought to survive in the few hours of sun the canyon bottom received.

As Gordy shoved into the open, he took time to take a breath, sitting on a rock to watch a water snake slither through the moss-lined bank. The canyon sides above, now devoid of major trees, were a blaze of white-flowered creek dogwood and twinberry near the bottom and smaller white-flowered chokecherry higher up where the rock was almost devoid of soil but still moist in the deep canyon.

He almost rose to climb the rock fall, but decided to try and pan a scoop first. He found a flat boulder and dug deep near its upstream side until he felt bedrock, then brought two handfuls of pea gravel and sand up, dumping them into his pan.

Almost immediately, color showed. Gordy began to tremble even before he had sloughed the lighter material out of the pan.

His mouth grew dry as he stared at the remnants left there—one nugget alone would go a half-ounce. He must have had twenty or thirty dollars gleaming in that single pan.

With a fervor, he continued to pan until he had several ounces of flakes and nuggets. It was the middle of the afternoon before he moved back from the creek and found a small clearing at the base of the boulder fall where he made a small fire. Then he sat and contemplated his new wealth until he had climbed atop the flat rock and yelled his joy.

The cry echoed up and down the narrow canyon, disturbing the warblers and flycatchers nearby. They winged higher up the canyon sides, relinquishing the bottom to the loud man who danced on the rock. They too enjoyed the deep canyon, for insect life—their pouch of gold—swarmed prolifically there. A small slate-gray bird, a dipper, ignored the man, and dove into the water near him, running along the bottom underwater, with wings half spread, collecting underwater insects until it surfaced, shook off the droplets, and flew into the willows. Then, scolding him, he cried a piercing zeet-zeet-zeet call.

Gordy laughed aloud, deciding he was the only one in the canyon who gave a damn about the gold—the birds and animals there mined for a more basic purpose, life itself.

Well, they would have to make way for him, at least until the gold was gone.

Gordy hefted the small leather pouch, already an eighth full, then tucked its tail into his belt and started the long trudge back to the horses. He would figure out how to block the canyon with poles where it narrowed to a natural gate, then return to his spot with a pack of supplies.

Billy would be fine with Clint Ryan and his friends until he got back. Even though Ryan might be angry at first, all would be forgiven when he showed them bags and bags of gold. Hell, he would even pay the man for watching his son if he was too upset.

A hundred yards above the creek bottom, an equal distance from the narrow spot where he would build his fence to keep the horses in, Gordy spotted a stand and deadfall of lodgepole pine. He would trudge up and drag some deadfalls down.

Then return to his crevice of gold.

All morning the exhausted men moved along behind the baying dogs, deer brush, manzanita, and wild roses grasping them. Finally, in a clearing surrounded by a solid green wall of lodgepole pine, Zeke plopped down next to a trickle of water and dug some jerky out of his knapsack.

He did not say a word to the men who joined him—no one spoke, for it required effort to do so. First Mort sank in exhaustion. Then Obe caught up, and he too fell to the grass, not even bothering to eat. Before Sam caught up, Obe was snoring. The red-bearded man stumbled up and sat where he could lean against a pine, then held his head in his hands.

"I never saw such a bunch of shirkers," Zeke muttered, his mouth full of dried venison. He gnawed the mess until he got it wet enough to chew, then, getting no comment from the others, cocked his head and listened for the hounds.

"We'll stay here a half hour, then move on. This time, he'll turn . . . he's leaded down . . . he'll turn."

"That devil will never turn," Mort said. "We oughta give up on that Satan and load up. We can make a pass by that pilgrim's place and pick up those horses on the way out. . . . That was the best idea you had since Tennessee."

"He'll turn."

"Never."

"Shudup and rest," Zeke said. Even he was too tired to argue, not that it mattered, since Mort, too, had fallen asleep.

Twotoes rumbled out of the lodgepole pine thicket onto a wide flat of digger pine and sandpaper scrub oak. He had been fighting the steep slope for an hour, his insides a ball of fire, his right foreleg sending a stab of pain up to his shoulder with every fall of his paw.

And still the hounds gained on him.

But the flat was easy, and he could lope steadily over it. He ran into a fern-covered wet spot and paused to lap some water from a still pool there, then moved away to a carpet of pink blossoming owl's clover. He browsed enough to gain a few mouthfuls of the succulent flowers and greens, then heard the dogs, much closer now.

He did not want to leave the abundance of the meadow, and glanced back over his shoulder with annoyance. With the echo of the hounds almost on him, he broke and ran—but jolts of pain met his extra effort. He slowed to the more comfortable lope, threading his way through another stand of thick lodgepoles on the far side of the flat and over deadfalls. He jerked up short as the pines suddenly stopped and the flat dropped away, steep at first, then disappearing in a cliff. He worked his way out on a granite outcropping and studied the country below. He could see for miles to the valley beyond.

Twotoes snorted his displeasure, and turned back the way he had come. He paused at the edge of the rock and studied the thick lodgepoles behind him, then turned and faced the incline again.

No, he would not be caught on the open bluff—a steep downhill slope he would have trouble negotiating.

He moved along the edge of the pines before turning back again the way he had come. Quietly, staying in the deep shadow of the thick trees and deadfalls, he inched his way along, having to drop to his belly at times, until he lay in deep pine bough shadow, only a few bounds from the trail he had taken out of the meadow.

The baying of the dogs was very near, ringing in his ears, and the odor of them rode the wind, offending his delicate sense of smell.

A high-crowned Steller's jay drifted down from the pine above and perched on a dead limb not two paces in front of him. He cocked his crested head in disapproval, his sharp clack-clack-clack cry scolding the bear, as a ray of sunlight glittered off his blue-gray plumage.

Silently, seven hundred pounds of waiting hell ignored the bird, concentrating on the shaded, partially occluded trail.

And the dozen oncoming redbone hounds, slavering with fresh scent, exhausted from the night's labor but still fighting for the lead, did not heed the jay's raucous warning.

Ramón led the palomino around and around the smaller breaking corral until the horse followed willingly. Clint and Gideon had gone back to work on the barn, readying the adobe, mortaring a split plank plate atop its walls to receive the log upper floor.

Billy Jessup perched on the top corral rail to watch, until the vaquero stopped and motioned him over. Smiley lay in the dirt, outside the corral, snoozing in the early afternoon sun.

"You give it a try now," Ramón said, handing him the reata.

"Okay," Billy said, but his tone reflected no confidence. He took the braided leather and began to walk, glancing back over his shoulder repeatedly at the quietly trailing horse. Ramón ambled along beside him.

"Animals have much better senses than we do, Guillermo."

"How so, Mr. Diego?"

"This horse can smell things you could never smell and those big ears can hear things much softer than you or I."

The horse followed willingly, but still Billy nervously glanced back as if expecting the stallion to bite a chunk out of his backside at any moment.

"And I think," Ramón continued, "they can smell fear."

"What's fear smell like?" Billy asked.

"I don't know, young William. I can't smell it, but I think animals can."

"So?" Billy said, again glancing over his shoulder nervously.

"So, if you are afraid of an animal, he will know it and will never come to respect you. And if he does not respect you then he will not learn from you, and you can teach him nothing. Are you afraid?"

"A little," Billy admitted, looking down and refusing to meet Ramón's eyes.

"A little is all right. I don't think they can smell just a little bit of fear."

Billy looked up, encouraged.

Ramón continued, "So don't show your fear to him, Billy. No matter what."

"I'll try," Billy said.

As he turned his attention back to the horse again, a flight of blackbirds lit upon the corral's upright rails. Tired of snoozing, Smiley broke out from under the lower gate rail and bellowed his disapproval at the flock, who immediately took flight. The big redbone barked again and leaped high, playfully antagonizing the birds.

Billy yelled as the palomino sat back, then he was lifted off his feet as the horse reared. Ramón snatched the boy out of the air and dove out of the way of the horse's pawing forefeet. They landed ungracefully in the horse dung and dust of the corral and rolled back out of the way.

The palomino trotted off, dragging the reata behind him.

Ramón sat up and curled his arms around his knees while Billy, wide-eyed, tried to determine if he was hurt or merely frightened. He decided he was not hurt, and started to get to his feet.

"Sit awhile, young William," Ramón said. "That was not your fault, nor the horse's. He was not fighting the rope, only reacting to the dog."

Billy plopped back down, mimicking Ramón's position, facing him. "Damn ol' dog," Billy groused.

"He was being just that, Billy. A dog. Do not expect your animals to be you. Love and respect them for what they are, and for what they possess that you do not."

"Like what?"

"You can ride the horse, and use his great strength to take you places you could not go otherwise. The dog will love and protect you with his life, and defend your home."

"I understand. . . . Smiley was just being a dog."

"That is right, and he would not understand being scolded for it. Do not fear the horse, Billy. He could have stomped us into the corral dust if he wanted to do us harm." Then as an afterthought he added, "But also do not fear turning him loose when the need arises."

Billy laughed. Ramón was caught up in it, and he too laughed quietly and climbed to his feet.

"Get the reata, and lead him for another half hour, then get to your chores."

"Yes, sir."

The palomino trotted away at Billy's approach, but the boy easily caught the trailing reata in the limited space of the corral. Ramón slid between the rails to go and join the men at the barn, but paused a moment to watch Billy, now leading the horse with greater confidence.

He will do, Ramón thought, *Guillermocito, little William, will do just fine.*

Later, when Billy figured the half hour was up, he led the palomino from the breaking corral to the remuda corral, and turned him out with the riding stock, then started for the house to soak some beans. Smiley trotted along beside him, as happy-go-lucky as ever. Nearing the door, to Billy's surprise, the big redbone hound jumped in front of him and barked sharply, barring his way.

Billy drew up short.

"Get out of my way, you ol' fool," Billy said, and started around the dog.

Smiley bared his teeth, and snarled menacingly.

Billy, a hollow feeling suddenly flooding his stomach, backed away a step. "Smiley . . . ," he muttered, suddenly aware that the big redbone bear dog was snarling earnestly.

The redbone whirled and approached the board step to the house, taking up the classic slow-moving stalk of a hunting dog. He did not go to a three-footed point, but rather, sat his front legs stiffly and stared intently, his big ears hanging motionless at the side of his head, his eyes unblinking.

Billy approached slowly and studied the spot the big redbone, in his hound way, had pointed toward.

Coiled in deadly silence, the swamp rattler had found a place in the shade, his flicking tongue, as he tested the air for the dog's scent, the only movement exposing his well-camouflaged location against the step riser—directly in the path of anyone entering the house.

Smiley barked loudly, only two paces from the coiled reptile, and the snake came instantly alive. The grating rattle pierced Billy's backbone, and even well out of the snake's reach, he jumped backward—a primal reaction as old as man and reptiles.

But Smiley did not move, other than to increase the tempo of his sharp barks.

The snake raised his head, contemplating a strike at the dog, judging the distance, then suddenly retreated, slithering away into a hole near the wall of the house, exposing his three-foot length for only a moment.

Smiley turned, attempting to patch up relations with the boy by curling his lips with the expression that had garnered him his name, then trotted back to take up his position beside Billy, who knelt and hugged the dog.

"Thanks, Smiley," Billy whispered quietly, and the dog licked his face.

Twotoes let the first of the pack pass on the trail he had doubled back on; three dogs led the others by several paces.

As the main body grew abreast of him, he gathered his thick hind legs under him and burst out of the brush with a heart-stopping roar, and charged into their midst—teeth and claws flashing.

With a swath of his forepaw, he disemboweled a hound and sent it flying. It skulked deep under some deer brush to die. Another charged him and got too close, and he caught it with the remaining two claws on his left forefoot and swept it up into his powerful jaws, unmindful of the sharp teeth of two others who clamped onto his hamstrings. He felt the dog's bones shatter in his jaws.

Spinning, with the hound dangling loosely in his mouth, he slapped at the two at his rear but they darted away. He flung the limp body with a flick of his huge head and charged the three dogs who had led the pack and now doubled back.

Blood dripped from his mouth as Twotoes met them in the narrow tree-bordered trail and ran over the first, who disappeared under the big bear. He caught the second as it tried to turn among the thick stands of pine and crushed it to his chest. The dog yelped, then blood gushed from its mouth, quieting it. But others were on him from the rear again and he could not turn without rising—so he stood on his hind legs, his upper body disappearing in the thick coverlet of pine boughs. He spun as a half-dozen dogs ripped and tore at his lower extremities and soft underbelly.

Forced to drop back to all fours, he did so and the dogs scattered in front of him. He charged back the way he had come, blood and saliva dripping from his jowls, his growls mixing in a calliope's range of yipping and snarling and death howls, of dogs fleeing in front of him and crawling away as others worried him from behind.

Two of the fleeing dogs entangled and one stumbled as Twotoes passed, enabling him to catch it with a flick of his forefoot. It crawled away dragging innards. As soon as he reached a clearing, Twotoes spun again and tried to rid himself of the dogs who now clung to hips and hind legs.

But they swung with him, the momentum of his turn making them fly through the air. He swiped back at them with his forepaw and knocked two flying, then sat back on another, crushing it under his weight.

Now he ran in earnest, a half-dozen dogs dead or dying behind him. The others were content to let him gain ground as they licked their wounds or inspected those who had fallen—but the respite did not last long. Soon the baying began again, but Twotoes, cut and bleeding from a hundred gnashing teeth, took some pleasure in the fact it was not as loud as it had been.

He came to the steep slope again, then slowed, carefully picking his way down until the brush was left behind. He found a narrow trail on the face of the cliff, its soft spots cluttered with the tracks of deer, coyotes, and cougar, and followed it. The cliff face dropped away over a hundred feet to the canyon floor below. He came to a dark opening, stood, and let his eyes adjust, sampling its dank air with his nose, listening carefully—smells of lion, bobcat, coyote, and bats, and silence. Nothing told him that any of the prior occupants were present.

It was a place to hide and lick his wounds. They could only come one at a time down the narrow trail. He would have the advantage. He entered the cave, turned in its narrow confines, and lay amid the stench of guano covering the bottom. Quietly he began to tend the many cuts and gashes that he could reach, and wait.

Zeke Stokes stood surveying the scene.

Brush and grass lay askew, blood soaked the trail, one dog hung from the branches of a manzanita, its innards hanging below and touching the ground, where ants had begun their feast.

He pulled his eighteen-inch Arkansas toothpick and slit the throat of a suffering hound just as the other three men caught up.

"Looks like a hell of a fight," Obe said, managing a dumb smile.

"A hell of a loss," Zeke said, counting the six dead dogs.

"He did turn and fight," Mort said, "like you said he would."

"If I hadn't a' stopped for you worthless pieces of dog dung, we woulda caught up. We coulda had him right here."

Mort gave him a dirty look, but nothing Zeke could have said would have made him angry enough to fight. All he wanted was to sleep. He sank to a log and leaned his head against his knees.

Sam staggered up behind them and fell to the ground, not bothering to remove his floppy-brimmed hat or the knapsack he had strapped to his back.

"You piss buckets can rest here if you want," Zeke growled. "I'm going back in the meadow and find a spot in that soft owl's clover to take a little snooze. Maybe that ol' bear will lay up and lick his wounds. We'll do better after a night's sleep."

"A night's sleep, that's what we need," Obe muttered, and fell into step behind his brother. Mort climbed up and staggered along behind, but Sam Polkinghorn was already snoring amid the blood and offal, and gathering flies.

With the sun still two hours from setting, the three of them made camp, chewed venison jerky, and drank from the slow-moving seep in the meadow bottom. They, too, were asleep long before dark.

The first dog reached the cave opening.

Twotoes charged him from the darkness and with a flip of his forepaw sent him careening out into space. His howls echoed as he turned end over end, a hundred feet to the rocky canyon bottom below. The five other dogs turned in the narrow trail, climbing over each other, and fled, yapping and barking. It was not a good place to fight.

Twotoes lay very near the opening in absolute silence. Maybe the stupid dogs would come again, or even better, maybe one of the man-animals.

Far down the canyon, Gordy Jessup had backtracked to the needlegrass meadow where he decided to make camp. The horses were hemmed in with over an acre to graze, a trout-filled stream bubbled with cold clear water, deadfalls of dogwood and lodgepole pine and banks of driftwood offered firewood galore, and best of all, the stream was a trough of gold. Gordy's gold.

He leaned back on a rock and studied the leather poke, now half filled with gold nuggets and flakes. Hell, he had not even bothered to pick out the dust from the pans. He figured he had twelve ounces, maybe a little more. At sixteen dollars an ounce, that was two hundred dollars or more—for two thirds of a day's work. He was rich. Rich!

Nothing could keep him down now.

All he had to do was stay out of the way of rattlesnakes or a flash flood—and pan for his gold.

Six

S AM AWOKE with a start.
    Something was gnawing at his leg! He screamed but the sound didn't come, and leapt up. A flurrying in his face caused him to throw his arms over his head as he staggered back.

Then he realized it was a big bird—a turkey vulture—and its wingbeats brushed by him. He was revolted by the thought of the filthy animal on him, and more so by the odor of death and blood all around him.

Two skunks, ignoring him, fed on the entrails of one of the dogs, and a fox scampered away into the underbrush. A half-dozen ravens complained with raucous caws and reluctantly took wing as Sam brushed himself off, still shivering, repulsed by the fact the big vulture thought he was dead, or dying.

Above, more of the big birds circled. He judged the sky, trying to determine if it was early morning or just getting dark, then got his bearings and realized the dim sky lay to the west, dusk. Walking in a circle, he saw where Zeke, Mort, and Obe had moved away from the spot. The bastards had left him to sleep among the blood and crud of the battle while they had gone to find a better place to sleep.

He walked back to the spot where he had been sleeping, leaning against the pine, and picked up his Hawken. Then the thought came to him, crept over him like a quiet specter in this place of death—in the deep thickness of the lodgepole pines, he could approach their camp unseen and unsuspected. Now was his chance to get even with Zeke for his still-aching jaw and the headaches that had plagued him since he was hit. Then he could slip away in the deep cover unseen before Obe and Mort knew what had happened. He could make miles in the darkness before they could ever begin to track him—though he believed the lure of the thousand dollars or more the bear would bring would probably keep the brothers on the trail of the griz. Hell, they seemed to like their brother little more than he did. They would probably appreciate what he was about to do.

Carefully, quiet as the vultures circling overhead, he began to follow their tracks in the failing light. Finally he could barely make out the trail, but he surmised where they were headed . . . back to the owl's clover meadow where the little trickle of water and deep comfortable grass beckoned. They had left him, the dirty bastards. Maybe that stupid Obe and the ghoulish Mort would try to follow, then he could pick them off from a high ledge with the long-shooting Hawken. Hell, they were little better than Zeke.

Sam moved ahead, no longer even trying to track in the failing light. Carefully padding along an open rent in the thick pines, he kept a sharp eye out. The faint twilight increased slightly as he approached the unshaded meadow. Stopping at the edge of the now deeply dark forest, he studied the open area until he picked out the glow of embers, a dying campfire. Slyly keeping to the forest's edge, he crept around in a direction that would take him nearer the camp, yet allow him to remain in the cover of the lodgepoles.

Each pace he laid carefully in front of him, stepping over downed pines, trying to avoid spots of dead bark and cones and dry branches that would snap underfoot, staying to green grass and soft pine needles. Each footfall now took most of a minute, and as he grew nearer, he grasped the Hawken more tightly.

When he was as close as he dared get to the camp, he strained to make out the more rounded shape of Obe, his blanket thrown back since the early evening still held some warmth of day. Near him, also on the far side of the fading coals, the long slim form of

Mort lay atop his blanket, his distinctive high-crowned hat across his face.

On the side of the fire nearest him, another blanketed form lay —even though he could see no face, it could only be Zeke.

Carefully, slowly, Sam brought the long rifle up, cocking it half-way and waiting a full minute until he ratcheted it again, back to its full cocked position. With great precision, he studied the sights until he was absolutely positive he was aligned, centered in the upper torso of the sleeping figure. A chest shot from the big slug would take any man to the afterworld, even one as big as Zeke Stokes.

The roar of the big gun reverberated across the meadow and the flash of its muzzle lit the night—the blanket pitched then stilled. But Sam did not wait for the results of his shot. He ran back the way he had come, breaking through the boughs and undergrowth, unmindful of their clinging pull. He ran and ran until he had passed the place of death where the dogs' corpses were again being fed upon by a variety of scavengers, ran another hundred paces, then slowed to a walk when he reached the granite-lined slope on the other side of the lodgepoles.

He worked his way out onto a rocky outcropping, unable to see much in the darkness. Luckily, the night was clear, the stars beginning to shine, with a three-quarter moon rising in the east. He saw enough to know that he stood near an edge, that the forest floor gave way to a void, and flung a rock a few paces out in front of him. It was long seconds before it hit far below, clattering in the stillness. He backtracked his way along the granite flat at the top of the drop-off. Beginning to get frantic, he feared the retribution of Obe and Mort, who were probably out there in the darkness, fed by vengeance—and he cowered, trapped against a sheer drop-off. God, he hoped he did not have to backtrack the way he had come. They would be waiting for him. Fear fueled his retreat.

Finally, he found a trail leading at an angle toward the cliff. There was a clearing ahead, he could tell; stars lit the sky low behind the way he was traveling. He knelt and felt the depression where a thousand or hundreds of thousands of hooves and padded feet had trod before him. It was a virtual highway of a game trail. It would lead him safely away and he followed it quickly, euphoria flooding him, fear slipping away.

The uphill side of the trail steepened until it almost touched his shoulder; again he would have to tread cautiously. He stood on the actual cliff face. Carefully, feeling each footfall until he knew for sure he had solid ground, he crept along. But the wide path continued, even on the cliff side.

He inhaled a deep confident breath as he worked his way down the vertical face. He was going to make it.

Hearing a shuffling sound, an odd muffled sound of something soft brushing against rocks, he spun.

Even before a jolt of fear could rack his backbone, the rancid breath of an animal doused his face in dankness, then, as if the cave itself had collapsed in on him, the huge animal crushed him to its chest and enclosed him in its powerful tree-trunk-thick forelegs. His breath was gone from stifling smash of bone, muscle, and fur. He could not even scream as he felt the wetness of tongue and wide mouth close over his face. He was lifted off his feet.

Then all was blackness as the massive teeth-filled muscled jaw splintered his skull as easily as a coon crushes a sparrow egg.

The tall tan oak, Ramón had taught him, was good for many things other than the hardwood it provided for the saddletree. Billy rubbed his work with his palm, testing its smoothness.

The tan oak's acorns were excellent food, if they were ground and the flour leached as the Indians did. Its bark provided the chemical, tannin, that worked so well for softening leather gleaned from bullock, or hides from antelope, bear, and deer. Its wood—harder than the hubs of hell, Ramón had said—was used for all the hundreds of purposes hardwood was put to, including the fireplace.

And hard its wood was, Billy concurred, as he continued to drag the drawknife across it, gaining only tiny swirls of grain with each pull of the sharp blade. The shaping of the saddletree would take some time, and only when it was well profiled could he begin to cover it with leather so it would become the saddle he would use on the palomino—the horse he had yet to name. Even more than with Smiley, he wanted the palomino to have the proper name and he had helped fill the time while he led the horse around the corral, teaching it to lead and more important to trust its leader, by passing a hundred names through his mind—but none of them seemed quite right.

He worked the saddletree and ran more names over his tongue, but remembered what Ramón had told him—his backside would pay with years of saddle blisters if he did not shape the saddletree perfectly. He worked on with renewed vigor.

All of Billy's spare time was now taken up with either gentling the horse or finding the right raw materials to make horse gear. He followed the men around in the morning and evening, collecting the long mane and tail hair curried from the horses so he could weave it into a girth when Ramón taught him how. Earlier, he and Ramón had searched hard to find just the right shaped tan oak limbs—deadfalls that were well dried—to make his saddletree. But even before Ramón would let him begin shaping it, he made him build the drawdown stand that the saddle would rest upon while being constructed. The stand had been a simple affair; waist high, with a pair of angled planks tapering from the center out on its top —the same angles as the horse's back. It had a hinged lever between its legs that could be worked with the foot to accommodate the action that gave the piece of equipment its name and draw down the leather, forcing it tightly across the saddletree that would rest atop it. And even before he had begun that, Billy was drilled in the names of the tools he would use—edgers and spikes, nippers and punches, awls, shaves, and pliers. And he was cautioned that he would also have to make the glue, from the horse's hooves trimmings, and tan the leather itself.

It seemed a prodigious task, one that would delay the riding of the palomino until a time so far in the future that it seemed almost unattainable. But Ramón assured him that the horse would not be ready before the saddle and bridle were, and vice versa.

Billy was placated, but barely.

Still worrying him, a niggling feeling always underlying whatever he did, was the fact his father had not returned. Clint continued to reassure him that his father had probably found the mother lode. He would not return until he had his saddlebags filled with gold—but somehow, Billy continued to fear the worst. And when his horse was ready, he had made up his mind, he would go and find his father.

Drawing the knife carefully and getting a good roll of woodgrain, his mind went to more immediate things. Then he heard the suspended piece of metal on the porch ring, and he went to breakfast, prepared by Ramón, knowing he had earned it. He had already been working for an hour after he had brought in the breakfast wood for the stove and a bucket of water from the river.

Zeke moved quietly out of the lodgepole thicket at dawn and walked to the camp. Neither of his brothers was awake yet, and the dogs had all returned to camp and slept soundly just outside the small ring of fire and larger one of bedrolls.

He walked to the blanket-covered log and studied the evidence. A clean hole was blown through the blanket and the slug had buried itself deeply in the pine log. He had heard the shot during the early evening, and all the hundreds of times he had left a false bed to crawl to a less comfortable one deep in the brush had suddenly been justified. He had come to the edge of the pines and watched his stupid brothers get up and investigate the blanket and pine log, then listened as they heard Sam break brush getting away in the forest—then they simply went back to bed. He had elected to not chase the bastard while he was hot with believed success. He would let the heat of the moment wear off, let the son of a bitch grow fat with self-satisfaction, then grow unwary.

"The cowardly bastard," Zeke whispered quietly, eyeing the splintered pine log that could have been his breastbone.

He kicked Obe soundly in the ribs, who "oofed" loudly but rolled over and continued sleeping. Mort also snored soundly, a deep rhythm. Zeke walked over to Mort and nudged him with a booted toe. Mort quickly rose to a sitting position, shedding the blanket from his upper torso.

"You worthless lout," Zeke chastised. "A man puts a ounce of lead where yer brother's own body should have been and you an' this dunderhead just go on back to snoozin'."

"He runned off an' is probably still a'runnin'," Mort said. "Twasn't no sense a'chasin' 'im in the dark. We checked to see it twasn't ya'll."

Disgusted, Zeke kicked Obe soundly, the thump echoing across the meadow. "Get up, boulderhead, and make the coffee. We're a'gonna track that griz and finish 'im, then run that brindletop coward down and skin 'im out . . . alive."

"Gol' dang . . . that would hurt," Obe said, sitting up and rubbing the sleep from his eyes with one hand and his bruised ribs with the other. Laboriously, he lumbered to his feet and stretched. "Ol' Sam better be a'hightailing it."

"Shudup!" Zeke snapped. "Make the coffee!"

"I'm a'hurryin'." Obe looked sheepishly over his shoulder at his brother. He picked up his pace as he went for water.

Forty minutes later, they made their way down the trail on the cliff face, following the baying dogs, who this time ran right on past the entrance to the cave, their nose to the trail.

None of the men even noticed the entrance, nor the remnants there, some with splotches of bloody scalp and red beard, as they hurried after the baying pack, now only five dogs strong.

Once the dogs reached the bottom of the canyon, their baying changed to a higher pitch.

"They're onta something fresh an' hot as a Nashville whore," Zeke said hopefully. He stopped on the trail still forty feet above the canyon floor, shaded his eyes, and searched the flat below.

Suddenly, on the far side of the willow thicket lining the creek, the big boar grizzly burst from cover, his powerful hind legs throwing gravel behind him as he clambered up the escarpment.

"Damn," Zeke yelled, and flung the Hawken to his shoulder, cocking it in the same motion.

The bear was over two hundred yards from where they stood,

and gaining ground fast. Even before Zeke could fire, both Obe's and Mort's rifles boomed, almost as one.

One shot hit behind the bear, throwing up a pillar of dust, and the other, a half heartbeat later, spit rock splinters from just ahead of the bear.

"Take yer time," Zeke cautioned, and carefully laid the sights of his rifle in line. Then his Hawken roared to mimic the other two. It spit smoke and drove his shoulder back, but this time the bear's forefeet went out from under him and his nose piled into the boulders. Zeke thought he had him, then as quickly as he had gone down he was on his feet again, spinning and heading back to the cover of the willows.

The big bear swept another dog away with the flick of a forefoot as the others closed around him.

"Don't shoot!" Zeke yelled. "We can't afford to be losin' another damned dog." The four dogs left were the worst of the lot, the least aggressive.

But it could have gone unsaid, for by the time they had reloaded, the bear had shaken the dogs and disappeared into the willow thicket.

"I hit 'im good. A killin' shot." Zeke began to move on down the trail as soon as he had tapped his wad into place over a fresh load in the Hawken.

"Maybe," Mort said, giving Obe a doubtful glance.

"We're right behind ya, Zeke," Obe called out and moved away after him, but Mort's caution made him move just a little slower than he might have. By the time they caught up with Zeke, he was scrambling up the escarpment to where he had hit the bear. He bent over and studied a spot on the rocks, then turned and came back down. Even though they could hear the pack disappearing downstream, both Obe and Mort continued to study the willow thicket that ran the length of the canyon, just in case the wounded griz doubled back as he had done before.

Zeke extended his hand, showing them some fresh red liquid spotting his fingers. "Good blood, not lung blood, but a lot of it.

We got 'im now. That som'bitch is carryin' a pound a' lead what with this an' what we put'n 'im last time. No critter is that tough."

"Should we oughta wait awhile? Let 'im lay up and get stiff," Mort suggested.

"Hell with that," Zeke snapped, and trudged off.

Speaking low so Zeke could not hear, Mort turned to Obe. "It might be to hell in a hurry—with Zeke and maybe all of us. If'n we follow that ol' griz too close. He's still got plenty of fight left in him."

"He's a goner, don't ya know," Obe said, casting Mort a disdainful glance, then he hurried to catch up with Zeke.

Mort, who had no interest in visiting Hades quite this early in life, followed at a respectful distance.

Pound of lead or no, this was one tough ol' bear.

Twotoes shook his head as he ran, flinging frothy blood from his snout. The shot had hit high on his back and traveled down, nicking his right lung and lodging in the thick cartilage of his broad chest. Each step was an agony, and his breath was cut in half by a lung full of blood which welled into his throat and made him cough. Finally, realizing the dogs were well behind, he slowed.

He wanted a high place, a place to lay up and heal. A place with clean cold water and clover, or a cave like the one he had spent last night in. At least he was well fed.

Turning up the slope, he tried to climb, but that only made the pain worse. Instead, he stayed in the bottom of the canyon and continued to crash through the thick stand of willows.

Blood covered his forelegs and, though near blind with pain, he decided he must climb, so he did. Soon, in a high spot on the canyon's edge where he could see his backtrail, he lay beneath a rock ledge almost completely shielded with dogwood, and stretched out, placing his head on his forepaws. His only movements were the heaving of his back as he worked extra hard to breathe.

He closed his eyes, and was still.

·   ·   ·   ·

Clint paced the ranch yard, going from job to job. For the first time in his life, he was in a position where his effort was not concentrated on a single task. His responsibility was for the ranch as a whole, and while doing one task, he had to worry about others. The horses were well in hand, but the sheep were in the hills with his Indian shepherd, Pohawut, and Clint had not seen them in weeks. The hogs ran wild in the groves of sandpaper oak that covered the low hills, or *lomerías,* as Ramón called them, and cared for themselves. The only time he would see them was when he wanted to harvest a few.

But he wouldn't put it past the Stokes brothers to take either at will, should they come across them. The sheep wore ear notches, as did the older swine, but even that would not deter the Stokes brothers, Clint feared. And with the gringo attitude in California as it was toward the Indian, he knew what would happen to Po, as he'd nicknamed the shepherd, should he try and stand in the Stokeses' way. They would shoot him down as quickly as they would a coyote. They might shoot him anyway, just for sport.

Clint at first had hired a Mexican shepherd, and he had been a good man, having worked at Mission San Luis for most of his life. But he was a wanderer, and after only a short time, had wandered on. But Clint had had the foresight to hire Po as his helper, and the young Indian had been an apt student.

He had to ride out and warn his man to steer clear of the Stokes brothers and to come and fetch him should any trouble arise. He decided to look for Po and the flock up in the high country, as the spring grass had begun to grow in plush depth there.

Diablo seemed pleased with his decision. After years of being almost constantly astride the big horse, Clint found himself now going days without riding. Diablo snorted and pranced, then threw his head and pawed the ground while Clint saddled him. The horse was ready to get out of the riding stock corral and on the trail.

It took Clint the better part of the morning to pick up the herd's trail, then another two hours to track them up out of the piedmont into the edge of the green wall that rose above the valley. Po knew the country well; as a Kaweah Yocuts it was part of his tribe's watershed.

They grazed a mountain meadow with a bog where a small creek widened in the flat. It was knee deep in lush grass and rimmed by Jeffrey pine. Clint made a rough count from the hillside, as best he could see through the pines. The flock was almost two hundred now. He gigged Diablo and the big horse picked his way down.

As Clint approached, Po stood over the carcass of a stillborn spring lamb. Clint dismounted and pulled a small satchel of supplies from the back of the saddle. One of the advantages of having a Yocuts shepherd was his ability to live off the land, but still Clint provided him with flour, a side of bacon, and some beans on a regular interval when he was in the high country. Po greeted him with his rough Spanish.

"Buenos días, jefe."

"It is a good day, Po," Clint said and greeted the young Indian with a handshake. Clint kneeled beside the man as he worked, skinning the dead lamb. They talked as best they could with Po's limited Spanish and Clint's almost nonexistent Yocuts, while Po carefully laced the lambskin about another newborn as if it were a cloak.

Clint's admiration of his shepherd's skills showed in his grin as the mother ewe of the stillborn readily took the camouflaged lamb to suckle. Clint knew the adopted lamb must have been refused by his own natural mother, but now he would be saved.

Clint took the evening meal with Po, making him understand as best he could the potential danger of the Stokes brothers, then saddled and rode out as the sun dipped to the western horizon.

Diablo picked his way back down the mountain with Clint's complete trust that the big horse would take them safely home. It was near midnight when Diablo's pace picked up, and Clint knew they were nearing the barn.

He hoped his worry about the Stokes brothers would prove to be no more than that, worry.

But Po was part of his responsibility, and he was glad he had made the trip as he rubbed the big stallion down, gave him a nosebag of grain, turned him out into the barn, and found his way into the ranch house. The barn wall had another two feet of blocks up, he was pleased to note, and he noticed the drawdown stand with Billy's saddletree affixed to it. The boy was doing a great job.

A pot of venison stew was still hot on the stove, and Clint ladled out a bowlful before he sat it off the almost dead fire. With a content smile, he found the two biscuits left for him in the stove's warmer.

"Po doing all right?" Gideon's voice rang low across the room.

"Doing fine. Everything okay here?"

"Fine as frog hair," Gideon said, then yawned and was silent.

Clint finished the stew and found his bunk in the darkness.

Seven

THE NEXT MORNING, Clint stood atop the adobe wall of the barn, readying it for the log section, then paused to watch Billy. The boy sat a few yards away atop the vertical posts of the breaking corral, unaware of the attention being paid him as he watched Ramón work the palomino.

Clint felt battered by mixed emotions.

He was happy for the boy, who was joyous at the thought of a horse to ride, but he was equally unhappy with the boy's father, who was still missing. Even more so, Clint felt guilty because Billy made him think of the Indian boy about Billy's age who had been taken by the bear, and of the boy's father who had come to him for help. It had been the first time Clint could remember, in all his life, that he had refused a request for help—it worked at him like a kink in his back.

"You going to notch that log?" Gideon asked, "or stare off into those mountains and *wish* a load of lodgepole pine down here?"

Clint glanced over at his friend, also standing on the sill, adze in hand, wiping the sweat from his gleaming black brow. "We should head upriver tomorrow and find a load to float down . . . while the water's still high."

"Suits me, amigo. I'll be happy to be through working this mud heap. I'm ready to fit some fine logs together."

"I'd like to take Ramón, because we'll need the help, and leave

Billy here, because somebody's got to watch the place . . . but I can't very well do that with Gordy not back."

"Maybe you ought to consider hiring some Indians to help us out," Gideon suggested. "That way Ramón can stay on the place with Billy."

"Good idea. I'll ride on down to the Tule village—"

"Ton Tache, on the lake, is closer. Old Chahchabe will give you some men."

"True," Clint said, rubbing the stubble on his chin, "but the Tules are only a little farther, twenty miles as opposed to eighteen or so. I'll tell you the truth. . . ." Clint removed his flat-brimmed hat and wiped the sweat from his brow and strands of light-colored hair out of his eyes, staring off into the mountains as he spoke. "I feel a little guilty about not helping that Tule chief . . . Trokhud . . . not helping him out with that bear. I'd kind of like to see if they're still being bothered."

"Go on," Gideon said. "I'll cut posts while you're gone."

"You might as well ride along," Clint said, heading for the ladder.

"Suits me. Maybe we can knock down a little camp meat on the way."

Before the sun was hardly over the mountains, Clint and Gideon, each leading a spare horse, were on their way to the Tule Yocuts camp, leaving behind the promise they would be back by nightfall. The ride would be the better part of forty miles, and it would require a steady lope and a continual change of mounts to make the schedule they had set.

Twotoes awoke stiff and sore.

In the distance, he could hear what had caused him to stir—the hounds bayed, coming closer.

He eased out from under the rock ledge and pushed his way through the dogwood. He no longer bled from the mouth, but flies worried the wound where the big slug had entered his back and he did not like the smell of it, but he could not reach it to lick it.

Carefully, picking his way, he moved down the creek, staying above the willow line, standing every few steps to check his back-trail with his sensitive nose and listen for the dogs. He would have to take cover when they came into sight, for he had learned, if the men could see him, they could hurt him. Until then, he could make more time in the open.

With an awkward jerking gait—he favored his right foreleg because of the pain deep in his chest as well as the old wound—he hobbled down the canyon keeping between a hedge of dogwood and the willows. Ahead of him was a small lake where the stream had backed up behind a rock fall.

Twotoes stopped suddenly to test the air. Confused for a moment, he rose on his hind legs and scrutinized the situation again. The sounds of the dogs were upstream, but the smell of man came on the breeze, up the canyon from below. He surveyed the canyon wall, checking it on both sides of the creek. No crevice seemed to have a trail he could follow up and out. Besides, it racked him with pain to try and climb.

Again he tested the air and listened. He did not like facing the dogs, for they meant men also. He would be better off facing man alone. He continued to move downstream, skirting the lake and hesitating as he reached the natural dam of fallen rocks.

There the man-smell was even stronger. Cautiously, his small eyes darting, he crested the pile and searched the willows below.

Gordy had decided to pack up and head back home.

If he could call it home. Billy was there, and he had the responsibility to go and get his son—a thought that galled him. It was unfair that God had taken his wife and left him with a small son, left him to be both ma and pa. If he had more containers to stow his gold in, he would have stayed and worked the creek, Billy or no Billy. But he would have had to sew sacks from his shirt and he had no needle either. He had even considered removing his trousers and tying the legs to make a big poke, but somehow could not picture himself—a rich man—riding back into Ryan's camp with no pants on.

Now, with two pokes full of nuggets and flakes—the only containers he had—he could at least pay Ryan for the horses and for some more supplies, and return with Billy and most of his gold and keep panning for more.

There seemed to be no end to the shiny metal. He had marked each corner of what he had hoped approximated a twenty-acre claim with a pile of rocks, pacing an estimated 660 feet wide up the canyon walls and 1,320 feet long up and down the creek bed, but had no pencil or paper to leave the actual claim of mining right. He would return with one filled out.

After catching his riding horse, he returned to his little camp and began saddling the animal by brushing his back with a hand, at least making sure he had no burrs there, then fitting the blanket in place. The bay horse snorted and jerked against the lead rope. The pack horse, too, was stomping and snorting in the needlegrass nearby.

"Here now!" Gordy scolded the animal, who calmed for a moment. "You loco knothead." Gordy again hoisted the blanket up on the animal's back. He smoothed it, then bent to pick up the saddle in one hand and swing it up—when the horse whinnied and reared, lashing out with his sharp forehooves. Gordy jerked him down, but the stallion reared again, dumping the blanket, his eyes wide with fright.

"Whoa!" Gordy yelled. "Calm down, you hammerheaded fool."

But the stallion was having none of it, rearing and jerking Gordy close and catching him with a flashing forefoot. Gordy lost the lead rope and the animal trod across the blanket as he galloped away. The pack horse joined the retreat until they came to the barricade of logs and brush Gordy had built blocking their retreat in the narrow spot.

"You damned fools!" Gordy shouted after the two frightened animals, rubbing his chest where the hoof had caught him, bruising him badly. He turned to gather up the lead rope to go after them, when a low rumble he did not recognize stopped him in his tracks and radiated a chill down his spine as if an ice spike had been driven into it.

He cut his eyes up . . . and there, standing nine feet tall, a huge boar grizzly loomed over him from only paces away.

Saliva dripped from the animal's mouth. He growled in earnest, this time loud enough to stop Gordy's heart in midbeat.

Gordy's mouth went dry and his knees turned to water as the growl reverberated up and down the narrow canyon.

But the animal did not have time to finish his warning. As he threw his head and roared in fury, Gordy overcame liquid knees, turning on his heel and scrambling after the horses. Running as he had never run before, he matched their speed for a few yards, crashing through the willows, fear pushing him like a wildfire lapping at his tail.

His only weapon was a little single-shot belly gun deeply rolled in his blanket—but its meager load would be a mere irritant to this huge beast. He heard the crash of brush behind him and knew the bear was coming through the willows. He sensed its hot breath on his neck and visualized the flesh being torn from his back in great slabs.

To Gordy's surprise, the two horses ahead galloped back his way, and for a moment he thought he would have the chance to catch one. But they were only circling, giving themselves room to take a run at the barricade. They spun and galloped for the brush-and-deadfall wall he had built, then gathered their hindquarters under them and sailed over it, their hocks and hooves catching in the brush and tumbling them head over heels—but both quickly regained their feet then galloped away.

Gordy ran without looking back until he reached the impediment of the flimsy fence which he now wished he had never built. He raced up it, knowing the bear was right on his heels. Then his foot slipped from a moss-covered log and he plunged down into the tangle. He jerked madly, unable to free it, and looked back to see where the bear was.

Gordy froze. Fear paralyzed him. Even his breath stopped.

The bear stood on all fours, not a half-dozen paces behind. It too stood unmoving, eyeing him.

"I got a little boy," Gordy said, his voice cracking in his throat. "Go away," he squeaked. "It's not your gold."

The bear roared again, flinging its head, throwing spittle to both sides of its massive shoulders. Then, slowly, it rose until it again stood nine feet tall and looked down.

Gordy covered his head with his hands and crouched as deeply as he could in the brush, closing his eyes, waiting for the bear's massive jaw to close over him and its claws to sever him limb from limb.

He prayed, for the first time in years, really prayed to his Savior. His hoped-for Savior.

Trembling, Gordy heard the movement of the bear, then felt the moisture flood his inner thighs as he wet himself.

"Don't eat me, bear," he said, his voice trembling as much as his knees.

But nothing happened. He stole a peek. The bear was not where he had been.

Ever so slowly, Gordy raised his head and scanned back and forth, searching the brush, wondering where the bear could have gone. He frantically began to free his stuck leg from the brush.

Still no bear.

He tried to listen for sounds of the animal, but his heart pounded like a bass drum in his chest, muffling other sounds.

Stumbling out of the brush and deadfall pile, he looked around again, and tried to listen as his heart calmed to a steady triphammer from its mad roar.

Nothing. Then, cocking his head, he heard the yapping and howling of dogs. A pack of dogs? A pack? The thought of wolves flashed through his mind, and he ran for the bedroll and the pistol.

Had he been spared by the bear only to be eaten by a pack of crazed wolves?

He had the little pistol in hand by the time the dogs crested the rock-fall dam and started down, carefully picking each step, jumping from boulder to boulder. They were dogs . . . hounds . . .

not wolves. Gordy breathed a sigh of relief as the four animals padded past him. They gave him little notice, noses to ground, yelping and barking and baying.

Gordy flopped to a rock, put his head in his hands, and began to alternately sob and laugh madly as, he presumed, the dogs chased the bear away.

Finally, he wiped the tears from his eyes. He still had the gold, and his life.

He almost mouthed the thought, *What else could happen,* but he did not.

His life was wonderful again. The bear was gone, the dogs were dogs not wolves.

Then he looked up and saw the three men slip over the rock fall and start down—three wild-looking men, carrying Hawken rifles, knives the length of short swords stuffed through their belts.

He had help.

They were almost to him when he realized he still had the two pokes of gold hanging from his belt, and elation gave way to trepidation.

Clint and Gideon rode into the Yocuts village on the banks of the Tule River just after the sun crested in the sky overhead.

The Yocuts lived simply. Their village was situated in a grove of stately sycamore near the river. Woven tule mats covered willow-framed huts with two or more families sharing walls so the huts stretched for up to fifty paces, while only four wide. Bowls of steatite and granite were scattered about the camp where women squatted or sat grinding seeds and acorns. Baskets, some quite intricate, hung from natural hooks on the upright willows of the huts, where limbs had been trimmed to leave a four-inch stump. As Clint walked his horse among the huts, he noticed one small well-decorated basket with a hundred or more quail topknots—fine black one-inch-long feathers shaped like question marks—woven into its topmost warp, creating a fine fringe. It was a work of great patience and craft.

Hanging from nearby trees, granaries three feet in diameter and six feet tall, made of willow branches woven with tules, held almonds. Each one held several hundred pounds, alternating layers of acorns and bay leaves, which kept the insects and worms away.

The men carried short hardwood bows and coyote or fox skin quivers of headless but fletched arrow shafts, and smaller quivers which held foreshafts with various sizes of stone heads—some only a half-inch triangle of exquisitely worked obsidian for birds as small as quail and some four-inch-long tapers of razor-edged glass-stone for animals as large as elk. A few of the men carried four foot obsidian-headed throwing spears with two-foot atlatl throwing sticks to give them added arm length and thrust.

As Clint and Gideon walked among the dozen or so long huts, the tribe viewed them with curiosity. The women, bare-breasted, with strands of olivella shells about their necks, and vests of rabbit skin over short skirts of reeds as a small token of modesty, backed away, leading toddlers and carrying infants in woven backboards, giving the strangers plenty of room. A center hut, the *temescal,* had much stronger posts and beams of pine with substantial cross webbing of mud-packed willow branches. It was sunken into the ground two feet or more, and steam and smoke worked its way from cracks in its upper reaches and curled from a center opening in the fifteen-by-fifteen-foot sweathouse. It served as the social meeting place for the village elders, in addition to being an integral part of their religion and health care.

Trokhud emerged from the sweathouse, pushing an elk-skin covering away from the door, followed by two of the other elders. His customary vest of rabbit fur and carrying net of woven fiber had been set aside, and he gleamed with sweat, clad only in a skimpy skin loincloth.

The chief did not seem particularly glad to see them, but custom dictated courtesy, and with a few simple hand signs he soon had Clint and Gideon out of their garments and in the sweathouse—which smelled of a thousand years of men ridding the poison from their bodies.

To Clint's chagrin, Trokhud fed the fire in the center of the black-smudged earth with a few more oak limbs. The temperature outside was warm with spring giving way to summer, but the heat inside was almost unbearable. The Yocuts handed both of them clam shells, which must have been traded from the coast tribes just as the women's olivella shells were, and showed them the method of scraping the sweat away—a function immediately necessary.

Clint had been in the Chumash version of a *temescal* before and, bemused, tried to keep from laughing as he watched Gideon go through the same trepidation he had the first time he had participated in the Indian ritual.

A small boy entered and served them unleavened cakes of acorn flour, and they passed a gourd of water which Trokhud occasionally splashed into the rocks surrounding the smoldering oak fire, sending up billows of steam.

Finally, to both Clint and Gideon's relief, they exited the *temescal*. When he got his breath back, Clint concluded that he felt wonderful, revived and refreshed, and even the heat outside seemed to bother him little. So good, in fact, that the thought of building a sweathouse on Rancho Kaweah teased his mind.

Trokhud was reluctant to provide Clint with men, even though he offered a fair price of two horses for two weeks' work for four braves. Agreement was reached only when Clint conceded that if they came across the track of the two-toed bear they would hunt it.

Trokhud was one of the four men who gathered to follow on foot. Agreeing that the Indians would not catch up until the next day, Clint and Gideon set off at a lope.

They stopped only one time, other than to water and graze the animals, when Gideon rode up beside Clint and, without speaking, reached over, slapped him on the shoulder, and motioned for him to rein up. Below them a tule bog stretched out from the base of the hill they traversed. Gideon pointed to a spot over four hundred yards away shaded by a gnarled old cottonwood, and Clint made out a small herd of elk resting under it. They dismounted and took different routes through the tules, and together they dropped an escaping six-hundred-pound antlerless bull.

The going was much slower with each of the second horses

loaded with a couple of hundred pounds of hindquarters and loins of a tule elk—and saddlebags full of heart and liver. Each man had a heavy hide bundled and tied on the saddle behind him, adding to the load. They were forced to walk the horses the last five miles.

When they reached the ranch, just as the sun dropped behind the mountains far to the west across the Ton Tache, their successful hunt added fresh fried liver to the plates of beans and tortillas Ramón had awaiting them, and they all feasted.

Billy seemed strangely quiet during the meal, his only comment: "My pa still ain't back."

As usual, Clint placated him with tales of gold, but Billy was not buying it.

So he changed the subject, but tried to include Billy in the conversation. Tomorrow, if the Indians arrived in time, they would head upriver to find a stand of lodgepole near enough to the river to drag logs there, and soon, the barn would be completed—if they did not come across the trail of the two-toed bear.

And if they did, Clint had resigned himself to the fact that they would hunt the animal until Trokhud had his revenge and Clint his peace of mind.

And maybe they would find Gordy Jessup.

Eight

TWOTOES LAY ATOP the last high oak-covered hill, the last of the piedmont before the lower hills flattened to the valley, intermittently green and golden where flat marsh bogs intermixed with chaparral-covered semidesert. But he faced the high mountains wistfully. It pained him too much to climb, or he would have returned there. Pangs of burning agony kept turning him downhill, away from steep ridges that would strain his torn lung and ripped back muscles.

The man he had come across near the creek had run, and Twotoes had no interest in feeding on men unless he had no other alternative, so he let him escape. But the horses were another matter. Four-footed creatures, much like the deer and elk he had occasionally taken, he had stalked them for a few miles but they had outdistanced him. He just did not have the reserve of speed that he needed. Instead, he had found a big patch of owl's clover and fed until he was full, which took little as he had no real appetite. Then he continued to move, always downhill, always away from the baying dogs. The dogs had not pressed him, having lost heart for the fight.

Twotoes raised his head and tested the air. He could smell the water in the valley below. Water and mud would soothe the hurt in his back and deep in his chest. Pulling himself to all fours, he started off with the peculiar stilted rolling gait he had developed to ease the pain in his right side.

Downhill, toward the water. Downhill, the same direction the horses had taken.

Gordy waved at the approaching men. As they moved forward he recovered his pistol from the blanket and stuffed it into his belt. He backed away and, his knees still like jelly, sat on a log, casually dropping the pokes of gold out of sight behind it.

"What brings you way out here, pilgrim?" the biggest of the three said with a stained-tooth smile.

"Just having a look at the country," Gordy said. He rose and stepped forward to extend his hand. "Gordon Jessup . . . friends call me Gordy."

"Howdy, Gordy," the big man said, crushing his fingers in a vice-like grip. "Looks like ol' griz damn near sat down to vittles with ya'll," he guffawed loudly. Gordy did not quite find the joke amusing.

"Breathing right down my neck, he was," Gordy said. "Skeered the hell and all right out of me."

"I see that," the big man said, looking at Gordy's still damp trousers.

Gordy flushed and changed the subject. "You fellas got names?"

"Sure do. . . . What was it ya'll dropped behind that there log?"

"What log?" Gordy said, his face blank.

"The one ya'll was a'sittin' on."

The other two men moved to flank Gordy. He moved his hand to the butt of the pistol in his belt, but the big man's rifle butt flashed out and smashed into the side of his head.

When he awoke a few moments later, the three men stood nearby, studying something in the palm of the big man's right hand. The pokes hung from his belt under his ample girth.

Gordy struggled to a sitting position, grabbed for the gun in his belt, and found it missing. Then he noticed it, too, shoved into the big man's leather belt.

"That's my gold," he said with wounded indignation.

One of the other men, wearing a high-crowned hat over razor

features, took a few steps over to where Gordy sat. "You done lied to us, pilgrim," he snarled.

"How so?" Gordy asked defensively.

"You said ya'll was lookin' the country over, and here we find yer pockets fulla gold. Did ya pan that right here in this little creek?"

"Why, no. I panned that way up north but then the sand bar played out. I been lookin' for more goin' on months now."

The hawk-faced man pulled the butt of his rifle back in a threatening motion, and Gordy flinched.

"If'n ya'll don't want the t'other side a' yer face blacked, ya better fess up. Ya got that gold right here, didn't ya?"

"No!" Gordy managed before the rifle butt slashed across the other cheek. Blood splattered the log Gordy perched on. He did not pass out this time, but covered the smashed cheek with his hand as he sat back up. Red gushed between his fingers.

"This here pouch still has a bit a' water in 'er." The big man, who appeared to be the leader, glanced over at Gordy. "You put some a' this in here in the last few minutes."

The man ambled over, pulling the ugly long Arkansas toothpick from his belt as he came. He hunkered over Gordy, his massive shoulders hunched forward. "Pilgrim, the good Lord wouldn't take kindly to yer lying ways. I'm a' gonna give ya to the count of three, then ol' Ezekeal here's a'gonna start a'takin' yer fingers off one at a time—"

Gordy quickly crossed his arms and stuck the fingers of each hand into the opposite armpit.

The big man guffawed. "Gonna hide 'em out, are ya? Even ol' Obe here can figger out where you're a'hidin' 'em. Boys, hold his hand out here atop this rock so I can have somethin' to cut on."

The two others leapt on Gordy, and soon had one arm shoved up behind his back and the other stretched out with his fingers splayed on the rock. The leader picked a stem of needlegrass and ran his knife across it, slicing it neatly. "I believe this'll do," he said, flashing a wide grin that showed badly stained teeth.

He raised the knife.

"No . . . no," Gordy flinched, then quickly conceded. "I got it right here outta this creek."

"I knew ya would see it Zeke's way." The round-faced one spoke for the first time.

"Now yer a'bein' neighborly," Zeke said, grinning. "Let him go, boys."

Gordy climbed to his feet. He gained confidence and spoke with some enthusiasm. "There's enough for all of us. I've got this little stretch of creek staked out, but there's bound to be more above and below here. You fellas are welcome to neighbor up."

"Zeke Stokes is the name, neighbor." Zeke changed the big knife from his right to left hand and extended his right to shake.

With a twinge of relief, Gordy offered his hand.

Zeke smiled, taking Gordy's hand in his; then the big man jerked him closer and slammed the long blade hilt-deep into Gordy's stomach. Gordy stumbled back and stared down, unbelieving, at the grease-stained wood handle protruding from his midsection. The long blade lay buried to its brass hand guard.

"You've killed me," Gordy managed as he sank to his knees, covering the knife's grip with both hands and trying to pull it out. The initial shock of the deadly blow wore away, and pain coursed through him.

"Ya know," Zeke said casually to the hawk-faced one, "I never saw a man able to pull one a' those toothpicks outta his gut afore he died. That's a right fine weapon."

"I'll bet ya a twist of chewin' tobacky this one can do 'er," hawk-face challenged.

"Yer on."

The one with the sharp features bent over him as Gordy sagged to his back. "Pull, damn ya!"

And Gordy did try, but his strength faded as quickly as his vision, his hands slipped from the knife handle, and flat, lifeless eyes stared straight ahead.

"Worthless lout," Mort said. He reached down to give the knife a twist before he jerked it free. Gordy twitched and his legs kicked spasmodically, blood welled from the wound, then a fine film seemed to glaze his open, but unmoving, eyes. "Shoulda tried harder," Mort groused, dragging the blade across Gordy's shirt, cleaning it of his blood. Then he flipped it and caught it by the blade and handed it back to his brother. With disgust ringing in his voice, he mumbled, "I'll pay ya when we get back to camp."

"Horsecrap. A bet's a bet. Ya'll pay me now or ya'll join this pilgrim a'poundin' on the pearly gates." Zeke held the knife tightly in his hand and moved a half-step closer to his lanky brother.

"Ya could wait," Mort groused, digging in his pocket to pull out a half-twist of tobacco.

"That's only half," Zeke snapped.

"It's all I got."

"Then ya owe me a half-twist . . . no, a full twist 'cause they be interest."

"I'd rather owe ya than cheat ya outta it," Mort said, stomping away toward the creek.

"Fat chance a' that," Zeke mumbled as he bit a chaw off the twist. He gnawed it, got it bunched in one cheek, then turned to his other brother and motioned to Gordy's unmoving body. "Drag this pile a' crap far enough away that the scavengers'll get 'im. I don't want him a'stinkin' our new camp up." He spit his first stream of tobacco juice directly onto Gordon Jessup's chest, where it mingled with the blood.

"We're a'stayin' here?" Obe asked, a hopeful smile covering his wide face.

"Dunderhead! A stream fulla gold is better than any ol' griz, no matter how big he be."

"That's a fact." Obe bent, hoisted the man's heels, and began to drag the body away from the gold-filled trough and its cold, clear, bubbling brook.

Billy had labored long and hard over a name for the palomino, and finally decided on Tache, after the Indian name for the valley and the lake. He had only been to the lake one time, but was mightily impressed with the huge body of water in the valley bottom.

Clint had expected him to come up with a name like Thunder or Star, and was pleasantly surprised.

Ramón had the horse taking the blanket and an old saddle on his back, and a headstall with a *bosal* across his nose—having again repeatedly tied the animal head to tail and made him spin in his tracks, only this time after saddle and blanket were in place. He was pleased with the animal's progress. Tache had spent so much time blindfolded that he seemed pleased to have almost anything done to him, so long as he could see. Each night, after a hard day's work training, Ramón would tie the horse to a drag log in the corral, where the animal could move by lunging against the log, towing it a few feet, but that was all. Generally, he was restricted to the length of the reata.

Billy had finished the saddletree and, with Ramón's close instruction, was fitting and gluing its skirts of heavy bull hide, pulling them down tight with the foot pedal on the drawdown stand. Now everywhere Billy went he carried strands of rawhide which formed the beginnings of reins, and their weaving was becoming second nature to the boy. He also picked and sorted horsehair, gleaning it from fence posts and rails where the horses rubbed, but mostly from the curry combs that hung near the saddle racks.

Before he was through, Ramón had informed him, he would weave reins and headstall; a *romal,* or quirt, that would be attached to the ends of the reins; and a *bosal* that would become a part of another headstall used in breaking the animals, as it would cut their airways by pressure on the top of their noses rather than the more cruel metal bit in the mouth. He would also weave hobbles, and a *cincha,* or girth, which was mostly a four-inch-wide horsehair band. All this at first seemed an unattainable goal to Billy, but now, with eighteen inches of rein completed, his skill and confidence grew with each inch, and he worked with new enthusiasm.

And each hour he saw an improvement in Tache. The palomino would come to him when called—for at Ramón's advice, he always had a handful of seeds or bit of tule root to please the little stallion. Twice, when Ramón had said the little horse was almost completely worn out, he had allowed Billy to take him a taste of precious sugar in his palm. Now the palomino would nuzzle Billy's pocket, seeking his treat, when Billy teased him by not giving him the delicacy right away, and the horse would come at a run at the sight of a nosebag.

But best of all was the riding itself. Each morning, Ramón would send Billy after his own horse and allow the boy to curry, saddle, and bridle the big gray. The first morning, after teaching the boy the proper manner of saddling and bridling, he gave him a long lecture on horsemanship and the *la jineta* method of the skilled caballero. *La jineta* had come with Cortés to Mexico, Ramón explained. It was this age-old, tried and true Spanish method Billy would have to master. He would become a caballero, a horseman, and a gentleman—a man whose horse would understand the slightest touch of rein or spur, and who would never have to beat or mark his animal.

He let him ride his own well-trained gray so he could properly ride the palomino when the time came. At first his riding was confined to the breaking ring, but after he had proved his respect for the gray—which knew so much more than the boy—Ramón allowed him to ride to the oak thicket near the rancho, so long as he did not go into the tules that began in oxbows off the main river course a mile or so below the house. The tules were filled with bogs and quicksand.

The ranch was abuzz with activity. The Indians had come at midday, and Clint and Gideon had sharp axes and a small crosscut saw awaiting them, as well as packs prepared for four pack horses. Clint figured it would take two days to locate and two more days to drag the logs to the riverside, then another two days to shepherd them down the shallows and twists and turns of the Kaweah.

Things were generally going well at the ranch. Ramón and Billy worked with the palomino and at Billy's tack, Gideon and Clint were about ready to leave, only having to saddle and load the pack horses, the Indian help was there and waiting. But then the two horses Gordy had taken straggled in, lathered and panting. The riding horse wore a headstall but dragged a frayed lead rope.

Billy climbed tentatively off the rail and moved to where Gideon had captured the two animals. "Those are the horses Pa had," he said quietly.

"Looks that way, Billy boy," Gideon said, quickly adding, "I've had more than one horse run off on me. Your daddy is probably hotfootin' it home right now, a little embarrassed about being afoot but none the worse for the wear."

Clint walked from where he and the Indians were loading the pack horses, the concern obvious on his face. "No saddle," he said quietly. "Pulled loose on him while he was saddlin' up and ran off, most likely."

"Shall we backtrack them?" Gideon asked.

"We've got four men here that I'm paying. Ramón can ride out for the day and look for him. We're going hunting lodgepole pine."

Just as Clint finished, Ramón walked up. "I will find him and be back by sundown. These animals do not look like they have traveled more than a half a day."

"I'll go too," Billy said anxiously.

"Somebody's got to stay on the place, Billy," Clint said.

"Smiley can watch it," Billy offered hopefully.

"And you, young William, can watch Smiley."

"He's my pa," Billy challenged.

"True," Clint said, "and if you want him found, you'll stay here so Ramón can ride out and locate him. Besides, what if he walks in here and finds no one around. He might saddle up and go out hunting us."

Billy chewed on that a moment. "I guess . . . ," he hesitantly agreed.

"Then it's settled." Clint ruffled Billy's hair, then turned to Ramón. "We're going to follow the Kaweah upstream until we locate some lodgepoles or Jeffries close enough to drag down, and hopefully a cedar for shingles. We shouldn't be more than a day's ride."

"Tile roof would be better," Ramón groused, but Clint ignored the oft offered advice.

Clint walked over and swung up onto his big palomino stallion, Diablo, motioned to Gideon, who sat a tall dun horse, and to the Indians. In moments they were disappearing upstream, Clint and Gideon mounted and leading a packstring of four animals, and the Indians following on foot.

"Fetch the gray for me and that skunk-striped dun for your father to ride," Ramón instructed the boy. "I am going to pack a knapsack."

Billy, Smiley on his heels, ran to do as instructed while Ramón entered the house.

Within moments, Ramón stood at Billy's side, saddling the dun while Billy finished the gray.

"You are getting to be quite a hand, amigo," Ramón said as he checked the cinch on the gray before mounting. He led the big stallion in a circle to the left then to the right, as he had taught Billy to do in order to assure the animal had no folds of skin under cinch or latigo, then mounted.

"There is plenty of stew on the stove, little Guillermo," Ramón said. "Heat yourself up some and do not worry. I will return with your father soon."

"Before dark?" Billy asked.

"Odds are before dark," Ramón assured him. "But just in case I am not back, you eat some stew and cold biscuits, then curl up on my bed if you wish. Fork some hay to the horses in the remuda and take care of the place." Ramón eyed the boy with some reluctance, but spun the gray and led the dun out at a lope.

Soon, he, too, rode out of sight.

Billy turned to the dog and knelt beside him, scratching his ears. "I guess I'm the boss here now," Billy said, trying to assure himself as much as the dog.

Smiley raised his muzzle and licked the boy's face.

After a moment, Billy rose and went to the stack of wild hay and began to fork some over the rails to the half-dozen head of stock left in the remuda corral. When he finished, he continued to stare first at the trail Clint, Gideon, and the Indians had taken due east up along the river, then at the trail Ramón had taken southeast.

For the first time since Billy could remember, he was alone—except for Smiley and the horses.

He sighed deeply, then headed for the breaking corral, where Ramón had left Tache snubbed to the post that stood alone in the corral's middle. He untied the little palomino, led it back out to the big corral, and snubbed it to the drag log, then stood for a moment, wondering how he was going to spend the day.

He decided to braid his reins for a while. If Ramón was not back by mid-afternoon, he might just saddle up one of the other horses and ride out himself to look for his father. After all, he was the boss of the place now, and the boss should be able to do what he wanted.

Nine

TWOTOES AMBLED ALONG as best he could with the pain deep in his back. He generally followed the scent of the horses, not hurrying, stopping to water at several trickles and to browse on sprigs of fresh grass that grew in the water courses.

Long before he could see them, he smelled and heard the horses coming. But the scent was mixed with that of man. Twotoes shook his head violently, flinging spittle and growling low. He left the trail and had to climb a little—a particularly painful process—to reach a rock ledge where he could overlook the trail which snaked along the ravine bottom. Now he could see them coming.

One was with a man-animal.

Still hurting deeply from the short climb, Twotoes backed into the deep shadows of a low buckeye, lay dead still, and watched the approaching pair. He could easily spring forward and pounce with his great weight from the ledge onto horse and man, and he itched with the urge to do so.

As it drew near, the lead horse's nostrils flared and he suddenly bolted, fighting the man, who spoke sharply to him. Trembling, the horse continued. Then the trailing horse sat back against the lead rope and the man had to fight to calm him. The rider turned his attention back to the trail ahead, carefully studying the brush-covered hillsides, but before he spurred the horse the man pulled out a stick and held it carefully, a stick like the one that had spit fire and smoke at Twotoes and which he associated with the pain he now carried.

Twotoes slunk deeper into the shadows and let the nervous horses and rider draw closer, twenty paces, ten. . . . Then the pain in his chest overruled the anger he felt, and he let them pass unmolested.

When all scent and sound of them had been gone for some time, he continued down the trail.

After a while, he snorted, catching the scent of smoke, and again of men. He shook his head angrily and raised his head to test the wind. Yes, smoke and men, but also horses. The scent came from the direction he traveled. But there was more—water . . . and mud. Soothing mud. He could almost taste the odor of thick rotting bogs. He would move forward cautiously.

Soon he rested in a thick grove of sandpaper oak on a low hill overlooking the corrals and the three buildings beyond. He stayed in the brush for a long while, watching, testing the air, as the sun moved across the sky, watching a small man-animal and the many horses below. He moved away and circled the man-and-smoke smell, ignoring the horses, for he had a greater need, and moving to the bog beyond.

Finally, far from the offending odors, he found a deep mud wallow where rooting pigs had cleared the tules, and slipped into it, carefully rolling, coating the wound in his back with the soothing muck—a coating that would keep the flies and insects from pestering and souring the wound. Then he moved deep into the tules, ignoring the irate scolding of a flock of redwing blackbirds, and rested his massive head on his forepaws, and slept.

Ramón pushed the gray up into the piedmont, leading the dun and keeping his eye peeled for the backtrack of the horses Gordy had taken to the hills. It was mid-afternoon before he came to a spot far up a sycamore-lined canyon where a waterfall tumbled twenty feet from a thickly wooded ledge above. He reined up and studied the small ridge and the hoof prints and gouges where two horses had slid and stumbled to reach the flat. Nudging the gray forward, he dismounted and led the animals up the same narrow game trail until he crested the top, then mounted again and moved forward through a narrowing cleft below canyon sides lined with golden-cup live oaks—its bottom becoming more and more crowded with sandbar, or river, willows.

He reined up. Ahead, through the thick patch of willows, he could see smoke. A telltale tendril from a campfire snaked its way up between granite walls.

He staked out the horses and moved forward on foot, sure that he would find Gordon Jessup sitting beside the campfire, nursing hurt feelings and awaiting a hoped-for rescuer. But before Ramón broke out of the undercover, he heard voices. Gordy was alone, at least so far as Ramón knew. He picked his way through the thicket, carrying an old muzzle-loader he had owned for more years than he cared to admit, and checking the single-shot pistol in its sheath at his side. For some reason, caution stalked with him, and he was careful with his footfalls. Finally, he could see into a clearing ahead. Beside the fire sat two men. Ramón recognized them. They were two of the three who had ridden into the rancho looking for coffee—the men Clint had sent angrily packing.

Why would Gordy's backtrail lead to them? Ramón sank back into the shadows of the willows to think this through. Not coming up with a satisfactory answer, he decided to circle the camp and see what they were up to before hailing them—if he decided that was the wise thing to do.

He picked his way back out of sight of the camp, carefully waded the narrow creek, then began a circle that would take him up the hillside, concealed by buckbrush, and around their clearing. He had moved only a dozen yards when a flock of ravens broke the air in front of him with raucous cawing and beating wings.

He quickly dropped to his knees and listened.

If his disturbing the rookery had alerted the men, they made no sign of it. He heard nothing coming through the brush.

After a few moments, he moved on—and almost stepped on Gordon Jessup before he saw him.

Ramón reeled back in shock. The ravens had been at Billy's

father, but the gaping wound that had killed him glared up at him. He'd been sliced open like a butchered hog and left to the vultures.

Ramón clamped his jaw in anger, wanting to stomp into the camp ahead, guns in hand, and find out just what had happened, but that would not be wise. And to try to take Gordy's body with him through this thick brush would be a dead giveaway. No, he would have to slip out of here and go for help. But not before he covered the body. With his hands, he worked for the better part of an hour until he had a couple of inches of soil on Gordy and then cut some branches and laid them and a few rocks over his grisly charge.

Still fighting his anger, he backtracked quietly. When he was out of earshot of the camp, he began to move at a trot through the brush. He finally came to the clearing where he had staked the horses, and, short of breath from the run, slipped the musket into the rifle boot on his saddle and put a foot into the stirrup. A voice rang out of the underbrush before he could lift himself into the saddle.

"I could blow ya right inta Hades if'n I wanted. Just ya'll back on down now."

Ramón snapped his head around to face the man who had been missing from the camp—his big Hawken, cocked and ready, lay trained on Ramón's midsection.

"Back on away from that splay-footed gray nag . . . and fish that pistol out real careful with jus' two fingers."

"What is the problem, amigo?" Ramón asked innocently, without removing his foot from the stirrup.

"I don't have none," Obe Stokes said, a lopsided yellow-toothed grin covering his face. "Ya'll's the one with the problem, don't ya know. Now you back outta that stirrup . . . afore I blow ya out."

As the afternoon wore on, Billy grew more and more concerned about being alone.

He tried to busy himself with the reins, but the nervousness of the horses continued to distract him. The mares trotted back and forth the length of the big corral, neighing and tossing their heads, while the stallions, in their three separate corrals, whistled their anger and repeated challenges to an unseen foe.

Billy had never seen the stock act like this. Finally, they quieted. It was as if a specter had floated out of the underbrush and teased them, unseen and unheard, from the edges of the corral. Billy wanted to walk up into the brush, but Smiley barked at him in anger, much as he had when the snake had been coiled near the step. He had learned to trust the big dog's instincts, and returned to sit on the porch, tossing rocks into a bucket until he grew sick of the game.

"I'm tired of this waiting. This is no way to run a ranch," he scolded Smiley as if the waiting were his fault.

Two riding horses remained in the corral. One was a cobby old range mare that was mainly used for packing but in an emergency could be ridden, and the other was a little sorrel mare with an almost perfect star on her forehead and with four matching white socks. Much to Ramón's displeasure, Clint had been training the mare to the rein for a very special purpose. A Spanish don who lived on a rancho bordering the Sacramento River had a daughter who had caught Clint's eye, and he wanted the mare, perfectly trained, as a gift for her. No matter what the vaqueros and Californios thought, Clint knew a mare, not a hot-blooded stallion, was the best animal for a woman to ride—and this was a special woman who Clint didn't want to see hurt trying to handle too much animal.

Billy figured he, too, could handle the mare just fine.

He wouldn't go far. He would circle the ranch and see if he could find any tracks of what had been bothering the horses earlier. Probably a big old mountain lion had come a little too close to the corrals for the horses' comfort. Well, Smiley would run a mountain lion a dozen miles from the ranch if they came upon him. Clint would be pleased at them running the cat off, Billy knew . . . even if he might be a little tad upset about Billy riding the sorrel.

.   .   .   .

Clint studied the river as he rode east. He reined Diablo up around a pile of lichen-covered riverside rocks, looking back over his shoulder to make sure the two pack horses trailed without problem. Gideon followed, absentmindedly humming some old hymn. The Indians trailed far enough behind to keep out of the horses' dust.

Clint pulled a last year's buckeye nut from a branch he had to push aside to pass, and flipped it back over his head, catching Gideon perfectly atop his wide-brimmed hat. The old rotted nut shattered, but Gideon merely widened one dark eye and gave Clint a hard look as he stopped his humming for a second.

"Seems to be raining nuts," he said, his gaze raising to the clear blue above, "an' not a cloud in the sky."

"I was just feared you'd go to sleep and fall out of the saddle," Clint said, then chuckled.

"Not a chance. I'm like a wolf an' sleep with one eye open anyhow." Gideon grinned. He went back to his humming.

Clint returned his attention to the river. Each shoal and shallow would be a challenge for each log and he figured he needed to negotiate the better part of a hundred and fifty thirty-foot logs down the river out of the high country.

And high country it was. As the canyon began to close in on them and the shallow rapids grew more common, he studied the country that rose much more steeply ahead. A giant dome of granite intruded on the north side of the canyon a few miles in the distance—a dome that rose well over a thousand feet almost straight up from where its base touched the wooded canyon wall almost a thousand feet above the rocky bottom. Clint had never been much higher up the Kaweah than where they now rode, but someday he would climb that canyon and see what was beyond that great dome. But not this trip. He was there to find some lodgepoles or Jeffrey pines and shepherd them back to the ranch, to finish the barn. If he remembered right, there was a good stand of lodgepole up around the next bend. If so, they could be on their way back down the river in two or three days at the most.

He remembered right. The deep dark pine forest began only a hundred yards or so above the river, and the canyon below fell away at an angle that would make a good skid road. He reined up in a clearing lush with deep grass near a spot where the river pooled with an eddy and back current. It was a good place for the horses to water, near the work.

"This'll do," Clint called over his shoulder, swinging down out of the saddle. By the time he and Gideon had begun unpacking the horses, the Indians arrived afoot, and soon the grassy spot was a camp and the horses were staked at the meadow's edge.

They had only a few hours of light left, but they set out up the canyon with saws and axes over their shoulders and soon the deep cleft rang with the sound of axe striking wood.

Billy had the mare saddled and mounted, and with Smiley close behind, climbed the low chaparral-covered hill near the ranch. Carefully, studying the ground for footprints, the trio circled the brushy hilltop. Just as Billy figured he must have been wrong about the cat, Smiley began to work the ground with his nose, yipping softly. Suddenly he began to howl and was off through the brush. Billy spurred the little mare and she followed as closely as she could, busting brush as Billy ducked and tried to cover his face with one arm, fighting to keep from being pulled out of the saddle by the clinging chaparral.

Finally they reached the bottom of the hill where the brush cleared, but Smiley was a hundred paces ahead and running hard, calling the ancient song of his kind, only occasionally leaping above the sagebrush where Billy could spot him. Billy felt mixed emotions as the little mare pounded after the dog—a little frightened by the mad gallop, more so by not knowing what they followed. The boy had spotted some pad marks as they galloped past a patch of soft earth, and they looked bigger than any cat's. But the trail was circling the ranch and whatever it was might have been stalking the horses.

And he was in charge of the ranch.

The horses were in his care. He girded his courage as the mare ducked and dodged through a stand of scrub oak, then skirted some tall tules. Billy remembered that Ramón had told him *absolutely* to stay out of the tules.

Fighting for control, he jerked the little mare to a sliding halt. She blew and shook her head, flinging lather and stomping with impatience, wanting to continue the chase.

Far ahead, Billy could see flights of water birds rise and hear the exuberant call of the dog, his resonant call echoing out of the wet bottom land.

Maybe just a little farther, he thought. He would stay on the edge of the tules, not actually go into them.

He held the mare to an easy single-foot for a few yards, then she got the bit in her teeth, got her head, and began to gallop again before he could control her. Billy held his breath as she leapt a wide bog and charged through a narrow line of tall tules. Billy jerked rein with all his might—and jerked her under control, stopping her again. They sat a slight rise where sage-covered dry land rose from the bog, but were surrounded by tules as tall as the horse's withers.

"Damn you!" Breathing heavily, Billy cursed the little mare, then flushed a little as he knew he would have had his tail tanned had his father heard him.

The mare, winded, was more than happy this time to stand quiet and blow.

Billy cocked his head to listen to Smiley's distant calls, when suddenly they turned to growls and yips.

Then silence.

Nothing but the sounds of the birds. A loon's lonely call echoed over the swamp as Billy strained to hear. Had Ramón not told him what the keening sound was, he would have been terrified. But knowledge is strength, and he had been learning every day.

The little mare, knowing far more than Billy did, raised her head from grazing. Her ears tilted forward, and she began to shiver beneath him. Then she snorted and pranced nervously. Billy tried to quiet her so he could hear any sounds in the distance.

Her fear transmitted to him, and Billy's stomach churned as he tightened his grip on the reins.

A whisper of reeds.

Something was crashing at a run through the tules. The mare tried to bolt, almost sidestepping out from under Billy. He reined her tightly, using all his strength to keep her head tucked close to her neck. She stood, but her eyes and nostrils flared as the sound got nearer and she tossed her head trying to get the bit in her teeth.

Billy stood in the stirrups, trying to see into the thick bog of reeds.

Something big was coming—he could see the tops of the tules being knocked aside as something passed through.

The sound of running pads sucking at the mud and tules being crashed away filtered through the reeds.

The mare reared and Billy had to grab for the saddlehorn to keep from being thrown, but the horse danced and sidestepped and he lost a stirrup. He managed to slap her across the ears with the *romal* and she quieted just enough for him to regain the stirrup. Just as he did, Smiley burst out of the brush . . . and a grin lit Billy's face.

The silly little mare had been frightened by Smiley returning. Only the dog. Billy relaxed, taking a deep breath.

It had only been the dog coming back through the tules—then a wall of brown fury exploded from the bog, a bull-sized animal, all teeth, snarling and throwing spittle, smashed into the clearing not a dozen paces from Billy and the little mare.

Fear flooded him—and the little mare went straight in the air, twisting and kicking. Billy clung in utter terror.

There was no containing the mare, not that Billy wanted to. She bolted, flinging mud behind her, retracing the way she had come.

Billy hunkered low in the saddle as she pounded along, terrified that the huge animal's claws would sink into his back at any moment. The little horse gathered her hindquarters and sailed into the air, jumping the same bog they had leapt coming. Smiley, to Billy's surprise, passed them, his ears flat back, stretching for all he

was worth, and Billy could hear the bear pounding behind—
closer, he was getting closer. Gasps of breath, pads pounding on
the soft bottom land. Billy wrenched his head around just as the
bear reached the bog—then suddenly Smiley reversed his direction. Smiley and the bear hit the bog at the same time and the bear
slopped into the muck in hot pursuit of the boy and the horse. But
Smiley was having none of it and fearlessly jumped directly into
the face of the bear, which swiped at him with a razor-tipped
foreleg. He would have impaled the dog, but the bear's other
forefoot sunk deep into the muck, throwing him off balance.

It was only a glancing blow, but it knocked the dog flying into
the tules.

Billy rode on, yelling behind him. "Come on, Smiley! Come
on!"

The bear's attention shifted to Smiley. The snarling beast
lunged after him, roaring in anger, only to sink to his belly in the
muck. The dog, lighter than the bear, was able to scramble across
the top of the flattened tules, then he too sunk to his belly and
yipped in fear, knowing he was soon to be fodder for the ferocious
animal. Smiley lunged against the restraining reeds—and the bear
struggled closer.

Just when the bear got legs under him and managed to lurch
clear, Smiley freed himself. He gained solid ground, covered with
muck, racing after Billy and the mare. He was not baying, exhausted, his tongue lolling, but free and ahead of the terrible mass
of killing fury, teeth, and claws behind him.

With the bear roaring in anger and frustration, trying to free
himself from the restraining muck, boy, horse, and dog moved at
breakneck speed through the scrub oaks toward the log house—
running for their very lives.

They raced into the yard. Billy leapt from the saddle, jerked the
headstall off the mare, giving her a chance to escape, but had no
time for the saddle. Only fifty paces away, the bear burst out of the
underbrush.

Billy made a decision, either the house or the stronger and win-
dowless *matanza,* the slaughterhouse, but it had a barred door

hard for him to negotiate. He ran for the house with Smiley on his heels. The mare galloped away.

They crashed into the log dwelling and Billy slammed the door behind him.

He stared at the plank door for a moment, realizing that the huge animal could smash it away with a cuff of his powerful paw. Billy began to push the table against it.

Just as he managed to get the table in place, he, table, and pieces of plank door where flung back like leaves in the wind.

The bear filled the open doorway, his head whipping from side to side, his teeth gashing, his roars reverberating in the enclosed space as if God had struck the little cabin with thunder and lightning. One forepaw reached out, its killing claws swiping at Billy. Billy careened across the small room in fear.

Then Billy realized the bear was too big for the opening—his shoulders had jammed.

Smiley lunged forward, leaping high in an attempt to tear the bear's throat, but a swipe of paw smacked him across the room and slammed him into a far wall, his shoulder laid open in a row of four evenly spaced deep blood-gurgling gashes.

Gamely the big dog staggered to his feet; Billy realized the dog was about to charge again. He dove across the space between them, pinning the dog to the floor.

"It's alright, Smiley," he reassured the dog with surprising calm in his voice while the bear continued to thrash in the doorway, his roars filling the house and shaking Billy's backbone. The dog quieted, seeming to sense that the bear could not enter.

Billy hurried to the stove, opened the firebox and picked up a limb with a few small branches from the wood box. He thrust it into the leftover coals until it flamed.

With a determination belying his age and the situation, he crossed the room and waved the flaming branch in the bear's face, but it only served to enrage the intruder more. The animal fought even harder to cram his way through the narrow doorway. Splinters and dust flew from the frame, spittle and roars from the bear.

Billy scrambled to one of the beds and pulled away a flannel sheet. He grabbed a broom—a pole with sage tied about its end—and wrapped the sage sprigs with the sheet. Returning to the fire-box, he got it flaming with ten times the ferocity of the limb.

Broom and flaming sheet held as far in front of him as he could reach, he jammed them into the bear's snarling face.

With a roar that almost collapsed the little ranch house, the doorway was suddenly empty.

The bear had retreated.

Ten

BILLY SLAMMED what was left of the splintered door, stood the table on end and shoved it against the opening, ran to the closest bunk and slid it across the floor against the table, then hurried back to Smiley. The big dog lay on his side, bleeding freely from the wounds in his shoulder. Billy paused long enough to douse the remains of the flaming sheet with a bucket of kitchen water, then tore away some of the unburned remnants to use as bandages.

He tended the dog, talking quietly to him.

Outside, he could hear the bear going from door to window to door, scratching at shutters, examining each opening with studied care, hoping for a way to reach the boy and dog.

The men had taken all the rifles and handguns with them, and Billy was unsure he wanted to try and shoot this immense animal even if he had a weapon. He might only enrage it more. And he secretly feared that the bear could take the cabin apart log by log if he put his mind and massive brawn to it.

With that uncomfortable thought, Billy began to tremble. Sitting beside the wounded dog, he realized *he* was all they had. Smiley was out of commission. He had to keep his wits about him. Ramón and Clint would want him to keep his wits about him. His father would want him to keep his wits about him. Smiley was hurt, they were gone, and the ranch was his responsibility. But he wished Ramón and his father would return, or that Clint and Gideon would get back—but they said they would be gone for days.

Cautiously, Billy worked his way to the window and peeked through a crack in the shutters. The bear was still outside, pacing from house to barn. The single horse left in the riding corral was going crazy, and far beyond in the big corrals, the other horses whinnied in fear, bunched against the rail as far from the bear as they could get. The old pack mare left in the remuda corral ran from side to side throwing her head in fear, her eyes open so wide that white ringed the pupils, her nostrils flaring with each terrified breath. So far the bear had paid her little mind, intent on the house and frustrated by his inability to get inside to the boy and dog.

Billy, over most of his bout with terror and flush with the success of his first attempt at keeping the gargantuan animal out of the cabin, stripped a sheet off another bunk and readied a new firebrand. If the bear came back and knocked the table away, which he could easily do, Billy would scorch him again. He sat by the firebox, girded his courage with the fact he had won once, and waited.

The sun was low in the afternoon sky, and Ramón would be back soon, hopefully with Billy's father. Together they would show this old bear. He grasped the broom tighter in his small hands.

This ol' bear'll be a rug by nightfall when Ramón an' Pa get back.

Bound and gagged, Ramón lay facing away from the three men at the campfire, whose harsh voices rang through the narrow canyon over the babble of the stream.

"I swear, I donno why you didn't jus' split his gullet like you did the other one."

"Mort, if'n I were ya'll I'd keep my flapper shut," the man replied ominously. "I'm tired a' listening to yer yap."

Ramón turned his head just a fraction so he could hear better, then heard footfalls just before a booted toe smashed into the small of his back.

"Yer awake, ain't ya?" the rough voice questioned.

Ramón tried to roll over and was helped with a shove of a man's foot. The man leaning over him was the most thickset of the three through the shoulders, with broad features and a lantern jaw, a full head of salt and pepper hair, and tawny eyes like a mountain cat. He had been the one who slammed the butt of his Hawken against Ramón's head just after the other one, the pudgy one, had led him to their camp at gunpoint.

All three wore buckskins and stunk of grease, their hands blackened and unscrubbed. They had an obvious aversion to lye soap and water.

Ramón had no way of knowing how long he had been unconscious, but now his head throbbed fiercely, and fire roared through his veins—he was angry, and fighting to contain it.

"I am awake, gringo," he said, spitting the words.

"Yer that greaser from down the valley. The one what works with the nigger and that stingy blond-headed lout what wouldn't share a little coffee."

"I work at Rancho Kaweah. Why am I tied?"

"Mort says jus' go ahead an' kill 'im," the pudgy one said.

"Obe, you dunderhead, shudup and let me do the thinkin'," the thickset one growled, then turned his attention back to Ramón. "I'll be the one doin' the askin', greaser. Now I'm askin'. . . ." The big man's eyes narrowed. "Did ya'll see anythin' over in the brush there when you was a'snoopin' 'round our camp?"

"Like what?" Ramón asked with all innocence. He was certain that admitting he had seen Gordy's body would seal his fate. All they had to do was walk up into the brush and see that the body had been covered to keep the scavengers off, and they would know. But until then . . .

"I saw nothing but the smoke from this camp, which I was coming to investigate."

"Then why did Obe say you was a'goin' the other way?"

"You said it yourself, he is a dunderhead—" His comment was

cut short with a kick that drove a booted toe into his gut, and Ramón doubled, fighting to keep from passing out.

"Jus' kill 'im, Zeke," the tall thin one said.

"Mordecai, I tol' you I'm sick an' tired a' yer yap. I got plans for the greaser here."

"Shall I go on back to the meat camp?" Obe asked.

"Obe, you did good a'bringin' this one in. It was lucky you seein' him."

"I did good," Obe said, a grin covering his face. "I can shoot him for ya, Zeke."

"No, you got about as much brains as a turtle has feathers. The greaser is smarter'n he looks, an' you're a dunderhead," Zeke grumbled. All sign of appreciation left him as quickly as his tone changed. "I jus' said, I got plans for 'im. You get on back to camp and tell those shirkers we're still chasin' ol' bear and may be a couple of more days. Make sure they're still a'workin' at fillin' those hogsheads."

"I'll make sure." With a nod of his head he turned and headed for Ramón's gray, mounted, and rode away up the steep canyon wall.

"That is my horse the dunderhead rides," Ramón growled, then flinched, expecting another kick. But Zeke merely smiled and chuckled. So Ramón continued, "And what are these plans you have for me?"

"Shudup, greaser," Zeke said. "You might jus' make some tradin' material, if'n that Ryan fella has any regard for ya'll, which I doubt," and again Zeke kicked him squarely in the stomach, doubling him. Ramón felt like heaving, but fought it. He would not give these three the pleasure. Zeke laughed and went back to his seat by the fire. "You get back to pannin' for a little dust, brother Mort. I got some thinkin' to do."

Mort gave his brother a hard look, but picked up a pan and headed for the creek without saying a word.

The pile of logs grew on the sand spit near the river. The Yocuts had fallen into the work with a vigor that surprised Clint; Gideon and the chief, Trokhud, had a friendly competition going regarding who could branch a log out the quickest. The others did the primary cutting, Gideon or Trokhud the limbing to reduce the trees to the primary log, and Clint manned the horses and dragged the logs down the steep skid row. Later they would all stack the logs, adding to the pile near the river.

Near dark, the stacking was almost complete. Clint had retired to the fire where he was fixing supper for the six of them when he noticed a wisp of smoke farther up the canyon, maybe as far as three quarters of a mile, he figured. He made note of it and decided that he would ride up after the meal to see just what was up. It was probably an Indian encampment, but it could be the Stokes boys. If so, he would want to know so he could keep a sharp eye out. He was sure they were up to no good.

After the meal he rose and walked to saddle Diablo. Gideon eyed him for a moment, then he too rose and walked over as Clint finished currying the big palomino.

"You just gettin' the burrs off him, or are you planning on riding out of here?"

"I figured I didn't get enough exercise today, so I thought I'd take a little ride and check out the country up the canyon."

"I saw the smoke upriver. You want company?"

"You don't figure you earned some sit down time today? Hell, maybe I'm payin' you too much." Clint chuckled and adjusted Diablo's blanket.

"You pay a damn sight better'n my last employer." Gideon flashed Clint a grin, turned, and went for his horse. "So good, I think I'll see you stay in one piece. That might just be those Hawken-happy meat hunters."

"Not like Indians to use a green fire. I'll bet you your share of the next pie that's just who's sittin' around that smoke."

"No bet."

Within a few minutes, they had left the timber camp behind and were working their way upriver, carefully avoiding the rocks and the clanking ring of hooves on them. In twenty minutes, just as the canyon was beginning to darken, they sat in a sandbar willow thicket studying the commotion across the river.

"Even if you couldn't see their smoke a mile away," Gideon said quietly, "you sure as hell could smell these boys. That's the damndest excuse for a camp I ever saw."

"I'm surprised they didn't stink us out a mile downwind," Clint added, then studied the camp a while longer. "I don't see those Stokes brothers anywhere. Maybe this is someone else's camp."

"Whoever they are, they're just as bad. There're no dogs in this camp, so maybe the Stokeses are out hunting."

"They've got nothing for us, amigo. Let's just leave them be." Clint wheeled the big palomino away, and Gideon followed without argument. Shadows had given way to total darkness; they just let the horses have their head to find their own way. By the time they reached their own camp, the Indians had retired to simple willow huts they had constructed a few paces downriver.

Clint and Gideon unsaddled in the darkness and picketed the horses.

"How about a touch of the barley before we turn in?" Gideon asked.

"You mean to tell me you brought a bottle along?"

"Just a touch. . . ."

"Well, dig it out, Gid me lad." Clint slapped him on the back. They hunkered down near the embers of the fire, now almost burned away, and Gideon passed Clint a bottle he had dug out of his bedroll.

Clint pulled the cork out with his teeth. "You're handy as a pocket in a shirt at times, my friend." He took a long pull at the bottle.

"It'll wash the stench of that hunter's camp out of your gullet."

Just as Clint upended the bottle, a voice rang out of the darkness. "Hello the camp. Tom, Harold, it's me and I'm a'comin' in."

With the reactions of men long in the wilderness, both Clint and Gideon backed away from the fire before Clint answered.

"Howdy. Keep your weapons put away and ride on in, if you're alone. We got coffee and a little supper grub left."

"Where'd ya'll get coffee?" the voice asked in amazement.

To Clint's surprise, one of the Stokes brothers rode in as bold as you please. But as soon as he reached the firelight, and Clint stepped up to be seen, his expression melted to surprise.

"I thought ya was some'un else. . . . Now I know why ya'll gots coffee. Yer that coffee som'bitch—" Obe nervously rattled on, one hand resting on the Hawken sheathed alongside the saddle.

"I've been called worse," Clint offered, a hint of a smile in his voice, but wariness in his eyes. "You'd be wise to stop pawing that pig shooter. Where are your brothers?"

"Out . . . Out huntin'. I was just a'ridin' back to camp, all alone," Obe said, suddenly defensive. "Musta missed a turn in the trail."

"That's Ramón's gray." Gideon's voice rang out of the darkness where he had remained. Clint's face hardened and his eyes went cold as a banker's heart.

"Where did you get that animal?" Clint's voice rattled low in his throat.

"This horse?" Obe said, looking even more innocent—then he slammed his heels into the big gray, which charged directly at Clint. He had to leap the fire to avoid being overrun.

Obe Stokes got only a half-dozen strides on Ramón's gray before Gideon flew out of the darkness and knocked him from the saddle. Obe hit with an "umph" that echoed off the canyon walls. Like a cat, Gideon was on his feet, jerking Obe to his before the man could gain his breath, much less his composure.

"The man asked you a question," Gideon said, his voice as low and ominous as Clint's. As he spoke, he slipped Obe's Arkansas toothpick out of its sheath, leaving the meat hunter completely unarmed.

Obe stared wide-eyed at the big black man whose face was only inches from his own, then at Clint, who strode over to join them.

"Where did you get Ramón Diego's horse?" Clint asked quietly.

"I . . . I found him on the trail—" Again he grunted as Gideon brought a knee up into his groin. Out of the darkness, the Yocuts gathered around.

Obe turned a pale green color and sunk back to one knee. He caught his breath and managed to groan. "Ya'll didn't have no cause—"

"You haven't seen nothing yet, Stokes," Clint growled. "I'll turn you over to these Indians . . . and they're liver eaters."

"Liver eaters?" Obe looked around and realized he was surrounded by not only the "coffee som'bitch" and his black friend, but by four Yocuts.

"Liver eaters—and Mr. LaMont here enjoys cutting them out real slow so they can take their pleasure." Gideon took the clue and pricked Obe's stomach with the point of his own long knife.

Obe flinched and began to quiver.

"Now, Mr. Stokes, where did you get that horse?"

"I bought him."

"You want another knee, or maybe you'd like this blade—"

"I found him."

Clint and Gideon exchanged looks.

Clint shook his head. "The next time you open your mouth, Mr. Stokes, it had better be the truth. These Yocuts went to bed without their supper, and they're craving liver."

"I took him," Obe said quickly.

"You and who?" Clint questioned. He doubted that this man was capable of taking Ramón's horse, unless he bushwhacked him.

"Me and my brothers," Obe said, regaining his confidence. "An' if they hear yer a'botherin' me . . ."

"Why don't we go find them and tell them," Gideon offered. Again he pricked Obe's ample girth with the point of the knife.

"Where are they?" Clint asked.

"Hunting."

"And where's Ramón Diego?"

"They took him along with 'em."

"I'm gonna ask you where just one more time, and if you don't answer with a place, Gideon is gonna open you up like a barn door and fillet your liver. You boys ready for a little feast?" Clint asked the Yocuts, nodding his head vigorously. The Yocuts had no idea what he was talking about, but smiled and nodded their heads in return.

"No! They're jus' over that mountain in a little draw that runs down to the valley. Zeke, he said he wanted to keep that greaser and he's got him a'tied up."

Clint turned to Gideon with a worried look on his face. "That means Billy is all alone at the ranch . . . unless Gordy's returned."

"He the prospector?" Obe asked, realizing that his helpfulness was changing the attitude of his captors.

"Light-haired fella, thickset, with curly hair?" Clint questioned.

"That's 'im. Big two-toed bear et 'im," Obe offered as casually as if he was talking about the weather.

"A bear what?" Gideon asked, though he knew he had heard right.

"Bear et 'im. Big bear, two toes on his left forefoot." Obe got a very superior look on his wide face, satisfied he had remembered the bear and seemingly pulled off a successful lie.

Clint walked over to a pile of gear and pulled out a coil of hemp rope, then threw it to Gideon. "Tie Mr. Stokes up. He can lead us back to his brothers' camp at first light. We'll see if it was bear or bear hunters that 'et' Gordy, and we'll find Ramón."

Obe's expression soured.

As Gideon bound the complaining Obe, Clint walked back to the fire to sit and ponder. By the time Gideon joined him, Clint had made up his mind.

"One of us has got to get back to the ranch to see that little Billy's alright."

"I'll go," Gideon offered, "or I'll head out after Ramón. It's your call."

"You head for the ranch. If we're not there in two days, then see if you can pick up Ramón's trail or come back here and track us. I don't know what these Stokes boys are up to, but they've got another half-dozen well-armed men in that meat camp who make their living shooting . . . and we'll play hell fighting them all."

"I hope the rest of them are as dumb as this one. He couldn't hit a bull in the butt with a banjo," Gideon said with a chuckle, then rose and headed for his horse.

"You could wait till first light," Clint offered, but knew that under the circumstances he, too, would ride out right now, and he did not really want to discourage Gideon.

"Ol' horse'll find the way. His nose'll be headed home."

In a few minutes, Gideon was saddled. Clint offered him his hand, and a "be careful."

"What do I tell the boy?" Gideon asked. He did not want to have to tell Billy about his father—at least what Obe had said, that a bear had eaten him.

Clint thought a moment, then cautioned him, "We don't really know what happened, so maybe it's best to say nothing until we do."

"That suits me," Gideon said, and gave spurs to the horse.

Clint retook his seat on the rock near the fire. He worried about Billy, but more so about Ramón. It seemed it was too late to worry about Gordy. He wanted to ride out right now, but he had to drag Obe Stokes along, and the Yocuts would be traveling on foot over some tough territory. He had to wait for first light.

Morning would bring some answers. He walked over and checked Obe's ropes and was not surprised to note that he was well tied.

"You som'bitch, you better untie me," Obe groused.

"You keep your mouth shut or I'll gag you besides," Clint said, and Obe grudgingly obliged.

He headed for his bedroll, but knew he would get little sleep. He hoped Billy was alright.

Eleven

BILLY SAT BY THE WINDOW as the sun dropped behind the coast range to the west. The bear came and went and came again. He worked at trying to get into the *matanza* after the smoked hams and other meats that hung there, but the heavy door and thick caulked walls without windows foiled him.

I wonder if he'll try to get in here again, Billy worried as he watched the bear until it was too dark to see. One of the pairs of stallions had leapt their fence, breaking the top rail as they did so, and run off. The mare in the remuda pen still ran from side to side in a frenzy. She spun and kicked at the rails until her rear hocks bled freely, but still remained captive.

The bear had paid her little mind—so far.

Billy crossed from the window to where Smiley lay. He had managed to get the bleeding stopped, but the big dog remained very still. Billy reached out to scratch the hound's nose, and noticed how warm it was. The dog was feverish. Billy poured him a little water in a wooden bowl and the redbone managed to rise on his forefeet and drink gratefully.

"Don't worry, Smiley, I won't let that old bear in here. I'll burn his eyes out if he tries again." Billy's tone of confidence belied the fear knotting his stomach. The dog licked Billy's hand then lay back down.

The little mare in the remuda pen shrilled a neigh of utter terror —and again Billy was consumed with fear.

.   .   .   .

Twotoes had busily investigated the compound of buildings. He did not like the main house where the boy and dog had retreated and he continually licked his lips where the boy had shoved the fire at him and singed the hair away.

Fire was a thing he truly feared.

Many fine smells of meat came from the other man-animal den, but they were well contained inside and try as he might, he could find no way to get to them. It frustrated him and the odors whetted his appetite.

He turned to the penned horse. In the darkness, more suited to his fine sense of smell and hearing than the day, he moved easily about the rancho. He found the gate gave a little when he pushed on it. The horse whinnied in terror and backed up to the fence on the far side of the corral, trying to climb it with flailing forefeet, spinning and trying to kick through with its powerful hind legs—but to no avail.

Twotoes rocked back and forth, standing with all of his great weight against the top rail of the gate until it gave way with a snap. Clumsily, he flopped over the lower three rails.

Now he was inside.

The mare lunged from side to side on the far end of the corral, neighing and whinnying in shrill screams of fright, but there was no escape. Taking a path in the center of the corral, Twotoes moved slowly forward on all fours, sensing that the horse would try and pass him on one side or the other in order to jump the gate where he had broken away the top rail. Just as he reached the center of the corral, the mare silenced her cries, feinted one way, then broke the other, flinging dirt behind her churning hooves. Stretching her fine neck forward, she strained to pass the bear to freedom.

Twotoes closed the distance in two great leaps and crashed his good right forepaw across her outstretched neck as she tried to gallop past. She went down in a heap, sliding on her shoulder, her head canted at an odd angle as she piled in the corral dust. When she stopped, she kicked twice, then lay still.

The big bear rose on his hind legs and made a full turn, his less than keen eyes checking to see if he had any competition for the meal before him, and his very keen nose and ears working the wind for smells and sounds of any who might contest his right to this kill.

There was only the smell of the boy, dog, and hated fire in the house; the meat from the other building; and the horses in the big corral beyond.

He dropped to all fours, moved to the mare, and began to feed in the darkness.

Billy's stomach churned in fear as he listened to the sounds of the bear going after the mare. It was the most terrible thing he had ever heard. Then he remembered Tache, bound to the log drag in the corral beyond. Suddenly he hated Ramón for making him tie the little palomino to the log every night—hated him, but wished he would return. What if the bear went after the horses in the corral? There was no way Tache could get free.

"Damn you, Ramón Diego," the boy said aloud. Then the sounds of bone crunching in the darkness brought him back to his own troubles.

He bent his head and began to pray. "Please, God, I'm sorry about the mare, but let that old bear get good and full of her and leave us and Tache alone. I'll be good for a long time, God, if you'll do that. Thank you, God." Then as an afterthought he added, "And keep Pa and Ramón and Gideon and Clint safe and let them get back soon . . . and let Smiley get well real quick."

Still he could hear the sounds of crunching. He began to sing a song Clint had taught him, one that had been his father's favorite. He clamped his hands over his ears so he wouldn't have to listen to the sickening sounds coming from the remuda corral.

> Hey, it's goodbye Muirsin Durkin
> I'm sick and tired of workin'
> No more I'll pick the Brady's
> No longer I'll be poor.

> As sure as my name is Kearny
> I'm off to Californy
> 'Stead of pickin' Brady's
> I'll be pickin' lumps of gold

He forgot the words for a moment, then picked them up again, even louder.

> I said goodbye to Shamus
> And soon I'll be famous

Forgetting again, he hummed aloud before returning to the chorus.

> Hey, its goodbye Muirsin Durkin
> I'm sick and tired of workin'
> No more I'll pick . . .

Realizing the sound of crunching had stopped, he paused and listened. What if he attracted the attention of the bear? He decided singing was not such a good idea.

Nothing. He could hear nothing. It was almost better when he knew where the bear was and what the monster was doing. He strained to hear. Billy crossed the room away from the window and busied himself scratching Smiley's ears and letting the redbone lick his hand.

Anything was better than just waiting. Where was his father? Where was Ramón? He wished Clint and Gideon would come home early.

Where was anybody?

But even more important, where was the bear?

It was eerie riding in the darkness. The moon was not out yet and with only starlight Gideon could see very little. Still, the dun horse seemed to have every confidence and plugged on. There was nothing but game trails to follow, and unfortunately, the deer were more than a tad shorter than the dun and a hell of a lot shorter than the dun with Gideon astride. Each time the horse got into a tangle he would follow a game trail out, and Gideon would have to duck low in the saddle to keep from being swept out by the stiff branches of the scrub oak—and usually only after he had been poked by the first of the branches. He could see almost nothing.

Still, the dun plodded on.

They had been riding for hours. The moon was up and the night much brighter when Gideon decided he must be nearing the ranch. The country had flattened considerably and the river ran quiet. The outlines of giant live oaks and sycamores intruded into the skyline.

It could not be much farther.

Suddenly the dun stopped in his tracks. His ears picked up and he stood stark still—frozen, not a movement, his breathing the only sound. An owl hooted forlornly nearby, and still the dun didn't move.

"What's the matter, horse?" Gideon asked aloud, happy to hear a voice even if it was his own. The night ride had not really bothered him, but the talk of Gordy being eaten by a bear gave him a little discomfort. He had not been real fond of Gordy. He had not liked the way he treated his son, but that did not mean he deserved to die a terrible death.

He grew impatient with the horse and gave him a brush of the spurs. The dun leapt in place, but did not move forward.

"What the hell is the matter with you? Don't you want to get home?"

The horse nickered quietly in answer, turned his head, and looked behind them—which gave Gideon pause for a moment—then, seemingly satisfied, set out again.

"Crazy damned horse," Gideon groused, but he slipped the Hawken he carried from its boot and carried it across the saddle. "You've got me half spooked, you crazy cayuse," Gideon mumbled. "Can't be much farther now, so just you keep moving."

But the dun needed no encouragement. He strode out with new purpose.

.   .   .   .   .

Twotoes had eaten several pounds of the horse and felt satisfied. He made his way off into a riverside thicket and laid his head on his paws to sleep. In the morning when he awoke, he would return to the kill and feed again. He had tried to move the horse out of the corral but with his injured left shoulder and the pain still deep inside him, he had trouble trying to heft her over the railing. Finally, he covered her as best he could with the dust of the corral and left her behind.

He lay under a tall live oak in the tangle of wild grapes, a hundred paces away from the corral, near the river, content.

Just as he was about to sleep, he raised his big head from his paws and tested the wind. Man-animal-smell drifted on the night breeze, and not the same one he had chased from the tules.

And a horse, another horse.

He stayed perfectly still, listening, testing the wind. Soon, he could hear the quiet plodding of the horse's hooves.

He inched forward to get nearer the trail they approached on. They would be an easy few paces away. They were too near his makeshift den. He would kill for food and he would kill to protect his territory.

He lay in wait.

Gideon recognized a particular spot where a meadow widened and led almost to the edge of the river, and knew he was very close to the ranch.

The dun grew more and more nervous as they rode closer, and now pranced and had to be reined back. Gideon fought to keep the horse on the trail and moving, for he was tired and wanted the pleasure of his own bunk—and the reassurance of finding Billy safe.

Suddenly the dun spooked and began to buck, trying to shed himself of the man-load he carried. Gideon was the weakest of the riders, except for Gordy, but stayed in the saddle until he got the dun quiet.

"Now, knothead," he lectured, "you try that again and I'll give you a crease between the ears with this Hawken that'll go to the

grave with you. Now, you put your energy into gettin' me to the
ranch and I'll turn you out with a belly full of oats. Agreed?" He
spurred the dun and the horse moved forward nervously.

Fighting to control the animal, he rebooted the Hawken and,
holding a tight rein, let the horse single-foot the rest of the way to
the ranch.

Twotoes watched with interest as the horse bucked and reared
and tried to shed itself of the man. But his full belly convinced him
to stay where he was as the pair neared, then passed. Finally, he
could make out only their outline in the distance.

It was not until Gideon reined up in front of the ranch house
that he realized something was wrong there. He could just make
out the smashed door in the moonlight. He leapt from the saddle,
removed the bridle, and slapped the animal on the rump, sending
him to the meadow near the main corral where he was sure he
would stay, and charged into the house, knocking table and bunk
aside.

"Billy!" he shouted.

Nothing.

He found a lantern and managed to set a match to the wick.
The spreading light reflected in Smiley's dark eyes. The dog lay
bandaged, but his head was raised and he quietly watched Gideon's every move. Beside him on the floor lay Billy, fast asleep, his
heavy breathing testimony to the depth of his slumber.

How the hell did you two manage this? Gideon wondered as he
inspected the smashed door, but decided against waking the boy.
"I guess it'll wait till first light," he said aloud, then realized that
first light was only a couple of hours away.

He made his way back outside, still clutching the Hawken, and
found and unsaddled and grained the dun as he had promised.

Then with great relish he returned to the ranch house, found his
bunk, sprawled fully clothed, and was asleep in a heartbeat.

Ramón had awakened several times in the night to the sleeping
camp and his bindings, and fought his bonds, but to no avail. He
had been securely tied hand and foot, then hogtied, and could not

move to find even a sharp shard of rock to try and saw through the heavy hemp. His anger quietly seethed as his joints stiffened. Shortly after dark, after his brother was breathing evenly, Ramón noticed the one called Zeke get up and slip off into the underbrush, to return only a half hour before light. Ramón found it strange, and though he lay awake, he said nothing.

At dawn the two meat hunters arose and moved about the camp without speaking, making coffee, gnawing some jerky. Finally, the one called Zeke ambled over and nudged Ramón with a booted toe.

"Ya'll know how to pan?"

"I am a horseman, a caballero, not a mucker of mud and dirt."

"Ya'll got all those fine horses broke what was in the corral down yonder?"

"Many are broke to saddle and bit, many more to the halter. Are you going to cut me free? I need to relieve myself."

"That mean piss, greaser?" Zeke laughed.

"As you wish."

"I don't give a damn if'n ya'll ever passes water again', 'cept I need a man to do some pannin'. I'll cut ya free and even give ya a cup a' mud to drink—we're a'drinkin' coffee made a' scorched wheat, thanks to ya'll—but ya got to promise to work and not try and hightail it outta here."

Ramón merely stared at the man in quiet disbelief.

"In a couple a' days, we'll haul ya'll back down to that trash heap your man Ryan calls a rancho, and if'n we can't get the drop on that Ethiopian and blond lout, we'll see if'n he'll trade a few horses for yer ugly hide . . . an' all a' ya'll's coffee."

"A few?" Mort called from over near the small breakfast fire they had built.

"Shudup, Mort," Zeke snapped. Mort knew Zeke would only settle for all the horses and everything of value at the rancho, but Zeke didn't want the Mexican to know that. "Yer gonna show this Mex how to pan!" Zeke yelled, changing the subject. Then he turned his attention back to Ramón. "And if'n ya'll don't pan out two ounces by high sun, then ya'll don't eat, understan'?"

Ramón had decided the only way he could escape would be if he was freed from his bonds, so he would go along with these men— for a while.

"Yo comprendo, gringo."

"Speak American, an' don't call me no gringo 'cause I don't know jus' what that means."

"I said I understand. Cut me loose."

As Zeke pulled his big Arkansas toothpick and went after the hemp using the knife's point to loosen the tight knots, he offered a final warning. "I can get those horses with or without ya'll, greaser, so don't get any ideas about me not shootin' your ugly ass should ya'll try an' run away."

Within minutes, Ramón was calf deep in the stream with Mort, and by the time the sun crawled over the mountain, had already begun to collect some color.

Gordy Jessup had found his gold mine, a stream full of the yellow metal, and it had gotten him offered up as buzzard feed.

As Ramón worked the rocks and riffles of the creek, he glanced up continually, searching for a suitable route of escape, but the steep walls of the canyon would make him nothing but a good target should he try. The only route was up or back down the creek, and with the two of them with the long-reaching Hawkens, that was a fool's journey. He would have to wait.

And he had left little Billy at the ranch alone.

Billy awoke well after dawn, surprised by the succulent odor of bacon frying. He leapt to his feet.

"Ramón!" he shouted, anxious to tell him of his conquest of the bear, but got no answer. He ran to the open doorway and looked out. It was Gideon, not Ramón, who stood next to the remuda corral, his Hawken hanging casually in one hand. Billy started to run over, then remembered Smiley and went back inside to check on the redbone. The dog was awake, and rose to his feet with Billy's attention.

"You gonna be alright, ol' Smiley?" Billy asked, scratching the dog's floppy ears. He rose and went to the shelf and returned and filled the dog's bowl with water. As Smiley lapped gratefully, Billy hurried on out to the corral.

He ran to his friend, and to Gideon's surprise, leapt up and clung to his neck. Gideon caught him with his one free arm. After the exuberant greeting, Gideon sat the boy back down.

"You had quite a night, young William."

"Yes, sir. That was the biggest ol' bear in all this country."

"Musta been real big. He ate twenty-five pounds of that little mare last night."

Billy stared at the partially covered remains of the mare in the corral. "I know. Smiley and I had to listen to it from inside the house. It was terrible. I just knew he was gonna try and get inside again."

"How did you keep him out, Billy boy?" Gideon knelt beside the youngster.

Gideon had studied the sign the bear left. A two-toed bear—the same bear that Obe said had eaten Gordy. Billy prattled on as Gideon thought how strange it was that the same bear was here at the ranch, and had almost gotten Gordy's son.

"Smiley fought him until he got hurt, then I jammed a burning sheet in his face. He ran like a scalded cat." Billy managed a small laugh. "But the truth was, he couldn't get through the door."

"That musta been a little scary. You did good, boy. Where's Ramón, Billy?" Even though Obe Stokes had said his brothers had Ramón, Gideon harbored the hope he had made it back to the ranch.

"He was supposed to be back with my pa afore dark." For the first time in hours, Billy remembered Tache. "What about my horse?"

"I checked the other corrals. All the horses are alright. Tache dragged that log all the way to the far end though. He's a tough little stallion."

"Real tough," Billy said, relieved, then got another worried look. "Is that bear gonna come back?"

"Not likely in the daytime—"

"It was daytime when he chased us in here," Billy said, looking a little guilty.

"Chased?" Gideon remembered he had bacon on the fire. "Come on inside and you can tell me about it." While he forked the bacon around in the pan, he continued to question Billy. "Where did you come across him?"

Billy shifted from one foot to the other before he answered. "Down by the tules. We just went to the edge," he said, his eyes fixed on the floor in front of his feet.

"You outran that bear all the way from the tules to here? You must be quite a runner, Billy boy." Gideon furrowed his brows at the boy, knowing he was yet to get the whole story.

"I was horseback . . . on the mare Mr. Ryan's been trainin'."

"And where's the mare?"

"I cut her loose, Mr. LaMont. I managed to drop the bridle and she ran off before the bear got here. He was right on my tail when I made the house. Then he crashed right through that ol' door like it was nothin'."

Gideon decided there would be plenty of time for recriminations about the horse. Billy knew better than to saddle any horse without permission, but Gideon would let Clint, or maybe even Ramón, handle that one—if Ramón got back safe.

"Well, we got chores, Billy. Bear or no bear, there are things to do. I'm gonna figure out how to fix that door. You fetch some water. . . ." Gideon thought about that for a moment, then added, "Maybe we'll both fetch some water, but not until we finish this bacon and a little coffee."

Digging a well was one of the many things that needed doing on the ranch and they had been bucketing water up from the river until it was done. A big spring watered the horses in the main corral, and Clint had constructed the remuda corral so the trickle from the spring watered it on its way to the river. It was shallow and muddy and they did not use it for house water. Gideon did not want Billy going down to the river alone, at least not until they knew that the big grizzly was well out of the territory. Secretly, Gideon doubted if the ranch had seen the last of the griz. The bear had left the mare half eaten and covered—a sure sign he meant to return.

Gideon would bury the carcass right there in the corral later in the day, after he fixed the door—double planked this time.

Gideon had thought long and hard about the timing of Clint getting to where the fat Stokes brother, Obe, said his brothers held Ramón. Gideon had basically ridden around the mountain, following the river all night. Clint and the Yocuts and Obe Stokes would be going over the mountain. The spot Obe Stokes had described was much closer to the ranch than to the lumber camp, so it would be an easy three-to-four-hour ride. He could take care of what needed doing, then he would ride out to meet up with Clint and the Indians, and take Billy with him. It was the only solution, as he could not leave the boy here in case the grizzly returned.

Even with the carcass of the mare buried deep, the bear was likely to be back.

Gideon decided to turn all the horses out. It would be better to round them up again than risk the bear getting to them while the ranch was unattended. He chuckled to himself. Clint would be madder than a wet wolverine when he found he had to round sixty horses up again, but that was better than burying their remains.

After breakfast, Gideon and Billy set off to do their chores before going into the scrub oak thicket to follow the trail down to the river's edge. Gideon felt the bear would not be anywhere near the ranch, at least not until night—but he carried his Hawken, even for the short trip to the river.

But he would hate to meet that bear face to face in the thicket, even with the Hawken in hand.

Twelve

CLINT SET OUT from the lumber camp to find Ramón well before first light. The Indians were, as usual, afoot, and Obe Stokes was tied in the saddle of Ramón's gray, being led by Clint.

Once they climbed the steeper lower slopes, the canyon began to ease and the buckbrush began to clear. Had it not been such a serious mission, Clint would have enjoyed the ride. He looked back over his shoulder and studied the high country farther up the canyon on the other side of the river. The canyon remained steep and spotted with gray-green digger pine and scrub oak far up the wall. Just before the half-dome, it darkened with dark green Jeffrey pine and patches of manzanita, then the granite dome rose almost straight up more than a thousand feet before its granite shoulders rounded. Beyond that Clint could not see, but he imagined the dome flattened on top. What a view a man would have from there. He could see the country for hundreds of miles around. He planned to climb that dome someday.

By mid-morning they had crested the mountain.

Clint reined up and let Obe draw alongside. "How far now?"

"They's over those next three ridges . . . a few hours."

"Will we get there before dark?"

"Just. But we oughta make it."

"No harm had better have come to my friend Ramón."

"Zeke does what he wants."

"Not here he doesn't."

Obe began to laugh quietly, then broke into a loud guffaw.
Clint touched a spur to Diablo and jerked hard on the lead rope,
making the gray Obe rode set back then plunge forward.

"Careful ya'll, I'm tied here."

"I oughta be dragging your fat arse," Clint snapped, then
touched a spur to Diablo again, something he seldom found cause
to do.

Ramón quickly became deft at panning the yellow dust and picking the small nuggets from the gravel.

He continued to look for escape openings, but with Mort working beside him and Zeke continually watching him closely, he saw
no chance. Finally, Zeke, his ever present Hawken across his lap,
began to doze. As the morning sun climbed higher in the sky, then
peaked and started down, Zeke's chin occasionally fell to his chest,
only to jerk back up again.

Finally, Ramón decided the man might fall hard asleep if he had
a full stomach. He complained to Mort. "He said I could eat at
high sun, if I had two ounces of dust. I have well over that."

"We ain't got no *frijoles* or *tortillas,* greaser." Mort grinned
with a glance at the sun. "But my stomach's flappin' against my
backbone too." He stepped away from the stream edge and
turned to his brother. "Least you could do, thinkin' man, is build
up the fire so's we can grub down."

Zeke rubbed his eyes and stumbled to his feet. "You build it up.
I gotta hit the bushes." He started into the willow thicket carrying
the Hawken at his side, following a game trail upstream away from
the camp.

Mort threw a few twigs on the campfire then grabbed a greasy
iron skillet and a few pieces of salted venison side-meat from a
cache in a cotton haversack.

Ramón turned to see Zeke disappear into the underbrush, well
out of sight. He focused his attention back on Mort. "You going
to cook in that filthy pan, amigo?"

"You don't have to eat it, greaser. 'Sides, you oughta like
grease."

"If you're not going to wash it, I will . . . if it is alright?"

Mort pulled the big Arkansas toothpick from his belt to slice some of the side-meat into smaller pieces to fry. He paused and eyed Ramón carefully before handing him the heavy iron skillet, but the knife lay gripped in an upward killing manner in his hand. "Suit yerself. But I'm jus' gonna dirty it up again."

Mort carefully eyed Ramón until he got well out of striking range with the skillet, then turned his attention to slicing the venison. With no chance to get in swinging range before he reached the stream's edge, Ramón spun, and with a great overhand fling, sailed the skillet the half-dozen paces between them.

Mort glanced up from his work just as the skillet clunked off his forehead. He dropped to his knees, a stunned look on his face, blood forming a rivulet from the gash in his head.

Ramón leapt the distance between them in three bounds as Mort groggily struggled to raise the Arkansas toothpick still grasped in his right hand. But Ramón's booted foot smashed up under his jaw and he crumpled over backward.

Ramón scooped up the skillet by the handle and smacked Mort across the back of the head. The sound—a Chinese gong—rang down the narrow canyon. Madly he searched the camp with his eyes—where was Mort's Hawken?

But wherever he had placed it, it was out of sight and Ramón could not find it. He cursed himself for not planning better.

"What's goin' on there?" Zeke's voice called from the underbrush.

Ramón scooped up the knife and ran into the brush, hoping against hope that he could reach the horses, picketed in a clearing downstream, before Zeke returned. He broke brush as he ran, making no effort to be stealthy—his only chance was the horses.

Before he had made twenty paces into the willow thicket, the boom of the Hawken filled the canyon, reverberating off its granite walls. Ramón flung himself face forward into the soft earth, the big ball singing its death song, whipping the wind near his ear, even before he had heard the powder blast. As quickly as he hit the earth, he was up and running again.

Willows tore at his clothes and upper body, but he broke into the open meadow where the horses were staked. His gray was not there, but the skunk-striped dun he had brought for Gordy grazed contentedly, tethered on its eight-foot lead rope. If he could get away with their only horse, he would be in the clear. With a sweep of the knife, he cut the rope near the picket pin and swung onto the dun's bare back.

A brush blockade had been constructed across the narrow canyon, and Ramón used the tail of the lead rope as a *romal*, whipping the dun into a gallop in three leaps—riding directly at the barrier. The dun gathered his hindquarters under him and leapt just as a searing pain roared up Ramón's side. He had no idea how he managed to cling to the dun's back, but he did. Pure instinct kept him astride the galloping horse, but he slumped forward and hung on to the animal's neck, fighting to keep his balance.

After a few minutes of hard brush-busting galloping, with every grasping limb a danger to his precarious balance, he came to the spot where the creek formed a waterfall, dropping away twenty feet to the meadow below. The dun slowed to a walk then stopped of its own volition at the steep drop-off's edge.

Ramón slipped from the saddle, weak from loss of blood. He investigated the wound in his side. The big ball of the Hawken had torn through his lower left side, luckily missing ribs. He tried to remember hearing the blast of the second shot, but could not.

The wound looked strange, he concluded, then realized a piece of bowel protruded from the exit wound in his stomach. His very innards were trying to work their way out. Studying the strange sight, he noted that at least the intestine that showed was not torn and leaking. Carefully, Ramón tucked it back inside. The wound oozed blood, but not so much as he might have imagined—nor did it hurt as he would have thought. He removed his shirt and bound it around his midsection. He would find some wild rosemary to pack the wound with—if he stayed conscious.

Carefully, so as not to spook the dun, he removed the lead rope from its neck and deftly tied a Spanish hackamore to fit over the dun's nose and ears. Now at least he had reins, even though he had no bit to control the animal. But he had trained the dun, and he was confident he could control it with only the nose loop.

Getting onto the dun's back was a major job, as he had already begun to stiffen—and the pain came in an avalanche. The effort ripped at his insides like a red-hot poker.

He gave the dun its head and the horse carefully began to pick its way down the steep game trail to the meadow below.

Ramón almost blacked out during the descent, but managed to keep his concentration. As they started across the flat he studied the growth in the meadow, looking for rosemary, but saw none. The green of the meadow began to swim before his eyes, as if he was looking into a moss-filled whirlpool of the little stream.

He slumped forward, riding now only out of lifelong habit, a life more in the saddle than out.

Still, the blood seeped from the wound both front and back.

His last thought as he slumped from the saddle and slid to the meadow was of Zeke—was he following? Had he hit Mort hard enough to kill him? The sound of the frying pan gonging on Mort's head brought a slow smile to Ramón's face as he lay prone in the meadow, then it faded.

He must move.

Must get out of sight.

On his elbows, Ramón dragged himself to a patch of underbrush. Satisfied he was at least partially out of sight of any pursuer, he laid his head down and closed his eyes.

The pain seemed to slip away, and so did he.

Gideon decided they would leave after their chore was done, and the chore was a new one. They walked to the big corral and turned the horses out, removing the drag rope from Tache. As the little stallion pounded out of the corral, Billy choked down a tear. "I hope I get him back."

"We'll get them all back," Gideon assured him.

They kept only the dun Gideon had been riding corralled in the breaking pen and an old mare Ramón had broken for a pack animal. Gideon was sure the boy could handle her.

Now they needed water to leave for Smiley, whose three-legged hop would not allow him to keep up during the coming trip to the mountains—and the Stokeses' camp.

They got to the river without incident, filled the buckets, and started back, Gideon with his Hawken carried loosely beside him, a bucket dangling from each side of the shoulder yoke, Billy lugging one beside him with both hands. Smiley, bandaged and asleep, remained in the cabin.

Gideon moved hurriedly along the trail, pushing through the thick brush. Before he had time to react, the bear was on him, rising like a great black specter out of the scrub oak, a whirlwind of power.

"Run, Billy!" Gideon yelled, then tumbled aside with a sweep of the bear's powerful forepaw. Had it not been for the shoulder yoke, Gideon's neck would have been broken like a twig with the horrendous swipe of the muscled foreleg. One bucket smashed to splinters, the yoke gouged deeply from the passing claws. The bear had burst from the dark shadows of the heavy scrub oak, a mass of swift-moving fur, flashing teeth, and claws.

Gideon lay gasping, trying to catch his breath, without the strength to move until he did so. The bear rose on his hind legs, all nine feet of him, and studied the retreating boy for a moment, seemingly unable to make up its mind as to which man-animal was the greater danger.

Gideon caught a deep rasping breath, but in doing so drew the bear's attention. The Hawken lay a half-dozen steps away and the bear stood a dozen beyond.

As he lunged for the weapon, Gideon knew it was a fool's bet—but better him than Billy.

The bear reached the spot at the same time.

All Gideon could do was roll in a fetal position, protecting his vitals, his hands clasped around the back of his neck, his eyes clamped shut.

Our Father, who art in heaven, he began silently.

The bear batted him, rolling him over and over as easily as he would a saddle blanket. Doubled up on the ground, Gideon did not move. The bear stood behind him. It was all Gideon could do not to look over his shoulder. *Just a glance?* But he sensed making eye contact with the animal was the wrong thing to do.

With a horrible roar, the bear came down on him. Gideon felt powerful jaws clamp on his shoulder, the bear's nostrils close enough to his own that he could smell the creature's rancid breath. The heat of it seemed to sear him and the pain of the great jaws crushing down on his shoulder ripped down his backbone and up into his brain until he suddenly felt it no more.

With the ease of a dog worrying a bone, the bear shook him then dragged him a few feet. Gideon straightened limply as he was carried, but when the bear dropped him, immediately recoiled, knees to face, elbows tucked into his soft underbelly, his hands protecting the back of his neck.

The bear roared its disapproval, batting Gideon once more. But Gideon didn't flinch. He remained perfectly still. *Can I run? He can outrun a racehorse for a hundred yards.* Gideon remembered Ramón's words. *Lie still, damn your ugly hide, lie still.* He kept his eyes tightly shut, his mind racing.

The bear moved forward again and Gideon once more felt its breath on his hands, fingers interwoven on the back of his neck. *Don't like the taste of me, you bastard.* Gideon held his breath. He almost screamed as the bear ran a raspy tongue across the shoulder wound. Gideon's heart slammed so hard in his chest he thought it would burst, but he didn't move.

The bear snorted and moved away. Snorted again, and moved back. The breath again. The winds of hell caressed Gideon's back.

Then he heard the bear move away into the brush. Silence. *He's gone, please God, let him be gone.*

Gideon slightly straightened.

The response was immediate. A crashing of brush and a slap of the bear's paw that sent him rolling.

This time he didn't move. *Don't move, no matter what, no matter if he begins to chomp on you again. Just don't move.* The hot breath on the back of his neck, then down, down along his back. *That part tastes bad too, bear. Don't be hungry, bear, you just ate half a horse . . . you can't be a hungry bear.* The animal investigated every part of him, nosing his buttocks, thighs, and calves. Toying with him. Then he bit down on Gideon's right boot. *Lord have mercy, he's going to eat my damned boots. There's man-meat in there, bear. You won't like it! But don't go after Billy. Billy, don't stop till you get in the house. Did I tell him to hide in the* matanza? *I did, I told him to hide in the slaughterhouse if the bear came back.* He muffled a scream as the bear crunched down on his heel, then tried to ignore it. Think about something else, anything else. *Do as I said, Billy! Think, Gideon old man, think of something else. Think . . . but don't move a gnat's eyelash worth.*

Then it was gone. As quickly as it had come. This time Gideon lay still, trying to calm his breathing and his heartbeat.

How long must I lie here? Count to a hundred.

He reached it.

Count to a thousand.

He passed out long before he reached it.

"I can't believe I missed that Mex's back. That was an easy shot . . . an easy shot." Zeke stood shaking his head, disgusted at himself even though the shot had been over a hundred yards. He had run up the canyon side and waited until the Mexican came into sight, then carefully laid down on him with the second shot— and he seldom missed.

He turned his wrath on Mort. "You dunderhead, you're worse than that pig-slop-for-brains Obe. Only one horse left and you let the Mex ride off on 'im. Neither of ya'll's got the brains of a flea . . . hell, not even that much, of a damned nit." Zeke stomped about the camp, shaking the Hawken at his brother, who sat on the ground, his legs folded in front of him, elbows on knees, head in hands.

"I'm hurt, Zeke. Stop yer caterwaulin'; my head is throbbin' somethin' terrible and yer a'fuelin' the fire."

"I'm not gonna stand for it. You get yer lazy butt up 'cause we're a'goin' after that greaser. I got plans for him."

"Yer not gonna catch 'im afoot. Those Mexes ain't worth much, but they can ride." Mort looked up from his hands and gamely tried to rise. He made it to a crouched stand, then sunk back to his hands and knees. Zeke took a step and cocked back a foot to kick his brother in the midsection, when Mort began to retch, losing what little breakfast he had had.

"Yer a worthless lout," Zeke mumbled, settling back on both feet, deciding that his brother really was hurt.

Mort spit, clearing his mouth, then looked up. "I swear, that Mex broke my head good. I'm sicker'n a snake-bit mule."

"Then lay here in yer own filth. I'm a'headin' back to the meat camp to round up those worthless excuses for men. Then we're going on down and clean that horse ranch out, an' then we're a'gonna get back north, sell the horses and the meat we've packed out, and find out how to file a legal claim on this bit a' canyon."

Again Mort tried to climb to his feet, but again sank back, this time sitting on his backside in the grass. He returned his face to his hands. "Dizzy," he mumbled.

Zeke began to round up his gear. "Ya'll wait here and watch the claim. When we get the horses, I'll send Obe back up to get ya'll. Be well by then."

"Sure 'nuf, Zeke. I'll be well by then," Mort managed, lying back in the grass.

Zeke collected all the gold—the two pokes Gordy had panned and an additional one Obe and Ramón had collected. He packed it and most of the provisions in a knapsack.

Zeke moved off through the willows upstream. He moved at a determined pace, incensed that Ramón had gotten away with their only horse, angry at his two worthless brothers, angry that his plans had gone awry.

He had hoped to be able to eliminate both his men at the meat camp—he had planned to leave them afoot—and steal the Rancho Kaweah horses, but then maybe he could manage both at the same time. If they attacked the rancho, in the rage of a gunfight if it came to that, so what if a few of his men died. Shot in the front by the ranch hands or in the back by Zeke, what was the difference? Each one that died meant an even bigger share of the profit for him. They would need at least one other man to help them with the wagons and driving the horse herd north—then Zeke could get rid of even him before the Stokes brothers reached the gold country.

He might be able to tidy up this whole business in one afternoon's work—and if Obe or Mort could not keep up, then that was their problem. He had carried them long enough.

He headed north, up and over the mountain, knowing he would hit the river and find the camp somewhere upstream.

Thirteen

BILLY HID in the slaughterhouse. The heavy door swung out and latched from the inside. There were no windows in the little building but a slow fire burned in a tiny stone fireplace, providing the smoke that cured the meat, and there was a tiny bit of light from the embers.

His eyes burned. He shook with fear, more for Gideon than himself.

He wanted Smiley.

He wanted his pa to return from the mountains.

Where was Ramón?

Why didn't Clint get back?

He hated the dark, not knowing what was going on outside. How long should he wait? He wanted to go now. Maybe the bear had left, maybe Gideon needed help?

Maybe the bear had taken Gideon?

Billy curled up in a corner of the *matanza* and waited.

Clint picked up the pace when they started down the mountain. He wanted to make sure to find the Stokes camp before dark, wanted to free Ramón if it meant having to shoot the hell out of the Stokes brothers.

Obe Stokes seemed content to be led along. He hummed and whistled. The Yocuts moved along with ease behind the horses, each carrying a bow and fox or coyote skin quiver of arrow shafts as well as a small bag of foreshafts. One man carried a four-foot spear and an atlatl throwing stick to fling it with. Clint had seen the implement used only once, but with deadly accuracy. The heavy obsidian head of the spear was five inches long and glass-sharp on its edges.

They crossed the second ridge by mid-afternoon when Trokhud, the Yocuts chief, ran up alongside Clint. He motioned for him to come back to where the Yocuts had gathered.

Boot tracks led away from the direction they were headed. He signed to the Indians, asking how many men traveled. They scoured the hillside and came to the conclusion that only one man had passed.

At the top of the next ridge, Clint reined up.

"Now, where exactly is your brothers' camp?" he asked the bound Obe.

"Not more than a mile down creek."

"You're gonna ride real quiet, Mr. Stokes. If I hear one sound outta you, I might just let these liver eaters have you."

"These ain't liver eaters, these is jus' digger Indians," he challenged.

"They'll dig your liver out and roast it to a turn, but you won't know it because I'll shoot you dead if you don't ride quiet. Do you understand?"

"How about lettin' me ride on in ahead?" Obe asked with conviction, as if he believed Clint might. "I'll tell 'em you're a'comin' an' only want to take the greaser out, then they won't shoot."

"That's not going to happen," Clint said. "Now keep your mouth shut."

Finally, after three quarters of a mile working their way down along the rugged ridge top, Clint reined up.

"How much farther?" he whispered to Obe.

"Two hundred paces," Obe answered, a little too loudly to suit Clint's pleasure. Clint dismounted and untied the bindings that bound Obe's hands to the saddlehorn. He jerked the big man out of the saddle and shoved him under the dense growth of a buckeye. Pushing him down to a sitting position, he tied him to the tree trunk.

"We'll be back to get you soon enough," he said quietly.

"Zeke is gonna shoot enough holes in you that they can use ya'll for a sieve." Obe gave him an evil grin.

Clint took the tail of the hemp rope he had tied Obe to the tree with and made a pass around the tree and through Obe's mouth. The wide-faced man tried to avoid the line, but Clint forced it into place, binding his head tightly to the tree and gagging him at the same time.

He gurgled, but could say nothing.

"You look a little like one of the ol' bullfrogs from down in the tules, Mr. Stokes." Obe's eyes bulged, adding mightily to the impression. "You can probably catch a half pound of flies before I return . . . if I return. You better hope your brother doesn't shoot us full of holes, Mr. Stokes, 'cause who's gonna find you up here if he does? The skunks an' badgers an' crows will have a feast gnawin' your fat ugly hide."

To the accompaniment of Obe's gurgles, Clint remounted. The Indians watched with amusement. Clint did his best to tell them what he wanted by sign language, and soon enough they had separated and were circling the spot where Obe had indicated the camp lay. Two of the men descended to the bottom of the shallow canyon, staying in the cover of the willows, then crossed to the other side. Two stayed with Clint. He rode only another fifty yards, leading the gray, before he dismounted and picketed the horses.

Then they proceeded on foot.

As they drew near, Clint stalked quietly. Trokhud and one of the Yocuts skirted a small lake on its far side, and Clint and two of the Yocuts skirted it on the side they had ridden up on. Obe had indicated the camp was just below it, on the downstream side of a natural dam. The sun lay below the three-quarters mark in the afternoon sky, but they had plenty of light left. Finally, he could make out the campsite through the willows. Only one man remained in camp, and he slept.

Clint signed caution to the Indians and moved forward. Carefully checking each possible place another Stokes brother might be, he approached the sleeping man. But there seemed to be no one else.

He toed the man, then prodded him with the barrel of his revolving breech Colt's rifle.

"Lemme alone, Zeke. I hurt like all hell."

"It's not Zeke," Clint said and the man bolted to an upright sitting position. With a grunt of pain, he brought his hands to his face and lay back down.

"What's the matter with you?" Clint asked, keeping the Colt's trained on the tall lanky Stokes brother.

"That Mex whopped me a good one. Broke my skull, I imagine."

"He packs a hell of a wallop," Clint said, a satisfied grin crossing his face.

"With a skillet he does, when a body's not a'lookin'."

"Looking or not looking, skillet, fist, or boot—now tell me where he is."

"Rode off."

"Where's your brother?"

"Which one?" He made an effort to move, still lying back with his hands covering his face.

"The ugly one," Clint snapped.

"They're both dog-butt ugly to everyone 'cept the common mama we shared."

"I've got Obe with me. The other one."

"Zeke went back to the river camp and said he was headin' out up to Sacramento," Mort said. He took his hands away from his eyes to see if Clint believed his lie.

"That would be smart of him. However, I've come to believe you Stokes boys are a lot of things, but smart's not one of them."

Mort managed to sit up, and this time he looked around. The four Yocuts had also gathered in camp. His eyes widened. "Why don't ya'll go about yer business and leave a man in peace."

"Which way did Ramón Diego ride out?" Clint asked, prodding Mort a little harder with the barrel of the Colt's rifle.

"Don't be pokin' on me, I hurt bad enough."

"Which way?"

"Downriver. Now go on after him and leave me be."

"Leave you be? I might leave you hanging from a tree . . . one of those oaks up the canyon there looks about right."

Clint's gaze followed Mort's furtive eyes to a rolled-out canvas bedroll, and noted the long hump covered by the folded-over cloth. "If you're thinkin' about going after a rifle in that bedroll, I'd think again. But then . . . your head might not hurt so much with a new vent hole clean through it."

"You got no scrap with me," Mort snarled, but the voice lacked confidence.

"We're gonna go on and find Ramón Diego, and if he says not, then you're right. But we're gonna find Ramón for the answer to that question first. Get on your feet."

Mort tried to rise, then threw up, spat, and sat back down. "Can't. Sick."

"Then we'll make a drag for you."

"Horses," Clint said to Trokhud. The solidly built Indian jogged off.

Within the hour, Ramón's gray carried Obe and pulled a drag constructed of two young trimmed-out digger pines with cross braces lashed in place, with Mort's bedroll stretched as a liner. The Indians flanked it, helping the load over the rough spots. Mort groaned upon occasion, particularly when they faced the steep downslope of the trail around the waterfall.

As they crossed the meadow, he found even greater reason to moan.

"You men just going to ride on by?" a weak voice sounded out from the brush.

Clint gigged Diablo over to the thicket and stared down at Ramón, bloody, but not beat. Clint leapt from the saddle and kneeled beside him.

Ramón grinned, then winced in pain before he spoke. "An *hom-*

bre can hardly nap around here with all the caballeros clomping by."

"What happened?"

"I see you have got a couple of Stokes boys with you. I trust you have shot the big ugly one."

"They're all big and ugly, but no, I haven't shot any of them."

"Well, the *chingaso* shot me, so I am glad you have saved him for my reata. Soon I will drag him the length of the valley, before I hang him from a sturdy oak. . . . They killed Gordy. Gutted him like a hog. He's up the trail a ways. . . . I buried him the best I could."

"I suspected as much," Clint said, and his eyes went as cold and flat blue as a December sky. He rose and walked back to the drag. "Up, Stokes," he commanded.

"I can't get up. I hurt—"

Clint placed a foot in his side and shoved him off the drag into the dust and weeds. He lay unmoving, but his eyes said it all. Clint motioned to Trokhud, who followed him and hoisted Ramón. They carried him to the drag and gently laid him in Mort's place.

Then he walked over, untied Obe Stokes' hands from the horn, and without comment shoved him sprawling from the saddle. He landed hard on a shoulder with an "oomph."

"No call for that," Obe managed as he struggled to his feet with his hands bound and tried to brush the dirt from the side of his face and shoulder.

"Get up and in this saddle," Clint snapped at Mort. Trokhud helped him to his feet and into the saddle. Clint bound his hands, tied them to the horn, then tied his legs to the cinch rings so he could not fall off even if he wanted to.

"You'll pay for this, Ryan," Mort said, his eyes as intent as a hawk's, his mouth turned down in a snarl. "Nobody treats a Stokes like a dog."

"I treat my dog a damn sight better than I'll be treatin' you. You give me the slightest excuse to take my fists to either of you, and by the time I finish, you'll have to be dead a week before you start feeling better." Then he remounted Diablo and set out, leading the gray. "Keep up," he snarled at Obe. "I'm still tempted to let the Yocuts have you."

Obe glanced at the Indians whom he now walked among, and hurried his pace.

Soon the Yocuts had stopped to study a track. Clint reined over, attracted by their excitement. When he reached them, Trokhud look up in anticipation. It was the track of the two-toed bear, and though a few days old, it led in the same direction they traveled.

"If we come across him, we'll hunt him," Clint assured the Indian. The other three seemed less assured than Trokhud, but he moved forward with renewed vigor.

Billy waited until just before the sun went down before he left the *matanza* where Gideon had told him to hide.

Quietly, almost without breathing, he crossed the ranch yard and worked his way into the scrub oak. With every step, he expected to be attacked and devoured by the huge bear. By the time he was ten feet inside the oaks, his mouth was dry as corral dust and he knew the bear could hear his heart pound a mile away.

Gideon was where Billy had left him—unconscious or asleep. He breathed, but shallowly. Billy took his shirt off and ran to the river, wet it, then returned and placed it on Gideon's forehead.

"Feels right good," Gideon managed without opening his eyes. He pried a brown eye open.

"Billy boy." He smiled wanly, then it turned down at the edges. "Where's that damned bear?"

"I don't know," Billy said, scanning the undergrowth, "and I don't want to find out."

"Agreed," Gideon said. He tried to turn over so he could get his knees under him. He broke out in a sudden cold sweat and rolled onto his back. The ground around him was rust brown with dried blood. "I guess I lost a little blood," he said. His eyes closed again. "I'm weak as a two-day kitten."

"We better get you to the house . . . just in case," Billy cautioned, still searching the undergrowth.

Then the sound of breaking brush caused them both to freeze.

It got closer, and Billy searched for an oak big enough to climb out of the bear's reach. But they were all too small.

"Don't wait," Gideon advised, but Smiley limped out of the brush on three legs. It had only been the dog following Billy, clumsily stumbling through the brush, still bandaged around his shoulders.

"Let's get back to the house," Gideon said with newfound conviction, and Billy needed no encouragement. Tenderly, after he had located a stick he could use as a cane, Billy managed to get Gideon to his feet. With Billy on one side and the cane on the other, he stumbled and hopped along. By the time he reached the house, all he could do was collapse on his bunk.

"We forgot your Hawken," Billy said. "I'll go back—"

"No, Billy, to hell with the Hawken. I don't want you out there."

"Yes, sir," Billy said, but he worried about them not having a rifle. If Gideon went to sleep, he decided, he would go back and find it.

They needed a rifle.

Zeke had picked up what he was sure was Obe's trail, but it led to the lumber camp, where the eldest Stokes carefully studied the sign and put together what had been going on. Who else would be up here cutting lumber but the men from the ranch down below. And Obe's trail stopped there. Then all the horses struck out back downriver. Why hadn't Obe gone on to the meat camp?

Zeke Stokes stood in front of the five men left in the meat camp, his tone indignant and belligerent—and completely self-righteous.

"Obe didn't make it back . . . those bastards probably bushwhacked him. They came into our camp while we was gone and stole what little provisions we had. It wasn't enough the louts wouldn't share they coffee with ya'll. They had to steal our goods. I say we burn them out."

He searched the men for support, but got little in the way of encouragement. The Swedes listened with interest, the Missourians, as usual, remained stoically quiet.

"Over a few grubby supplies?" one Swede, Johanson, questioned.

"Not only a few supplies, they stole a horse. You fellows know horse stealin' is a hanging offense. Leaving a fella afoot is good as givin' 'im a death sentence."

"I don't know," Johanson mumbled, then his brows furrowed. Petersen, the other Swede, stepped forward. "The horses you boys rode out huntin' on came back to camp on their own. Where did you get a horse for those fellas to steal?"

"Traded a fella for 'em," Zeke said, stepping forward in a threatening manner. "You callin' me a liar?"

"Nope, just wondering." He backstepped to stay out of Zeke's reach, but he was not convinced. "I don't know about this, Zeke."

"Well, I know. They did us wrong. And they got sixty head a' horses at that there ranch. Ya'll ride with me, and I'll add those horses to the poke. They'll bring a hundred a head in the gold fields." The men searched each other's eyes, each of them looking for a sign from another. "That's about six thousand added to the poke, boys."

"I still don't know—" Johanson said. He and Petersen traded doubtful glances.

Zeke took another threatening step forward. "Any man who don't ride with me rides again' me, Johanson."

Johanson was no coward, but he had seen the fury of this big Stokes man more than once—and knew him to be just on the near side of crazy. He backstepped again, but he had another unanswered question. "Where's Sam Polkinghorn?"

"Sam got et by the griz."

That quieted the group. Finally, Johanson spoke up. "You're the boss, Stokes," he relented. "Let's get done what needs doin' and get on back to Sacramento City."

"That's more like it. Now bean up and bed down for a while. We ride when it's dark. I want to hit that pig sty in the middle of the night when they're unawares. We'll leave here just afore nightfall . . . an' we should be back in Sacramento City in a few days with our pockets fulla gold coin."

The men grumbled among themselves, but not openly. They ate and lay down to get a little rest before riding out.

Hunting deer and bear and antelope was one thing, but hunting men—that was a bird of a different feather. Still, six thousand in horses would double their take.

And as Zeke said, the men at the ranch were a den of horse thieves themselves. Maybe right was with them. Those ranch fellows were about to reap what they had sown.

Fourteen

THE MOON was well into the sky by the time Clint rode into the ranch. He was worried. He had not come across Gideon on the way—and it was not like Gideon not to do exactly what he said he would do.

He became even more concerned when he noted that there were no horses in the main corrals. Quickly he unsaddled Diablo in the breaking corral, as he had found the dead mare in the remuda corral where two other horses were contained, then he strode for the house. The Indians waited near the door with Ramón on the drag.

"Let's get him inside," Clint said.

Clint shoved the remnants of the smashed door aside.

"Get out, bear!" Clint heard little Billy's terrified voice ring out. A flare from the stove lit the boy's small face.

"It's me, Billy boy," Clint said, and a look of relief spread across the boy's features. He ran forward and hugged Clint tightly. "Where's Gideon?" Clint asked, kneeling and holding Billy at arm's length.

"Right here, Clint," Gideon's weak voice sounded from his bunk.

Clint got a lantern going and swung it Gideon's way. "What the hell happened to you . . . and that door?"

"Griz. Big as Hades itself and twice as mean."

Within minutes, after they got Ramón inside and the Stokes

brothers tied to the hitching post in front of the ranch house, Gideon and Billy had filled Clint in on the events since they had left.

Then Billy realized his father had still not returned. "You didn't find my pa?" he asked sadly.

The men exchanged a furtive glance.

Clint walked over and put his arm around the boy. "Come on outside, Billy. We need to talk a little."

"My pa's dead," Billy said, expressionless.

"Come on," Clint repeated, guiding the boy to the door. Outside, they walked away from the Stokes brothers. Billy had not known they were there, and he stopped and stared at the two for a moment, tied back to back to a hitching post, then followed Clint across the yard.

Near the *matanza,* Clint kneeled down in front of the boy in the darkness. "You're right, Billy. Your father was killed."

The tears began to well in Billy's eyes, then track his cheeks.

"But you've got a home here, son. Ramón and Gideon and I'll make sure you're well taken care of."

"How did it happen?" Billy rubbed the tears from his eyes.

"He was killed by those men, and their brother. We haven't found the brother yet, but we will."

"Aren't those the same men who left Smiley here?"

"Same ones, Billy."

The boy stood in silence, staring across the yard to where the Stokes brothers were tied. Then he broke and ran as hard as he could and began pounding Obe with his fists. Before Clint could stop him, Obe had managed to kick the boy away and send him sprawling in the grass.

"Don't let that whelp be hittin' *me,* " Mort Stokes said, doing his best imitation of a snarl, which melted away as the pain racked his head.

Clint got the boy to his feet and stood with his hands on the boy's shoulders. "I understand what you're feeling, Billy. I lost my ma and pa when I was about your age . . . a little younger, in fact."

"You did?" Billy said.

"I did. Now come on inside and let's get settled down."

A tentative voice called after them. "What about the bear what killed that horse?" Obe asked.

Clint stopped and glanced back at the Stokeses, who were beginning to feel a bit uncomfortable about being tied out in the dark with a fresh bear kill nearby.

"No self-respecting bear would eat anything as revolting as a Stokes," Clint said, continuing into the house. But he decided he had best tie them in the *matanza* before they turned in for the night.

Besides, a little smoke would serve to make them both smell better.

Clint had no trouble convincing the Indians to bed down on the ranch house floor. Like the Stokes brothers, they too had no desire to be outside near a fresh grizzly kill.

Twotoes moved away from the oak thicket and the river and out into the tules. The wound in his back was hot with fever and festering, and he sensed he needed the mud bog again.

He rolled in the muck in the darkness, then lumbered away and found a particularly tall tule patch, wallowed until he had a clearing to his liking, then laid his great head on his paws to rest.

It would be hours before the pangs of hunger came to him, and he knew where his next meal was.

He drifted into a deep sleep.

Zeke Stokes rode with determination, the five remaining meat hunters following with varying degrees of enthusiasm. They tracked the same basic set of game trails Clint and his timber seekers had used to come upriver and Gideon had returned on. Up the side hills to avoid the tangles of brush and vine along the river, but always following its course out of the canyon.

A sliver of a moon helped guide them, but it was still two hours before dawn when they reined up a couple of hundred paces from Rancho Kaweah, the Ryan ranch.

"Let's get them horses rounded up an' moving on up the trail. A couple of you can drive 'em, then the rest of us'll put fire to the buildings an' pick 'em off like ducks as they run out."

"I don't know—" Johanson began, but Zeke cut him off.

"You an' Petersen take the horses if'n you don't have the sand fer it. The rest of us'll take care of the horse thieves. Now shudup . . . I don't wanna hear another peep outta ya'll."

They moved down the scrub-oak-covered hill, picking their way carefully to the main corrals. Zeke stared in confusion at the empty open spaces. He found a gate, dropped its cross arms, and rode into and around the big corral in the darkness, refusing to believe his misfortune. Nothing.

He returned to where his men waited.

"They're gone. Not even a whinny left." Zeke rubbed his whiskered chin. "Maybe they sold 'em off," he concluded. "If so, they got a sack fulla money in that house. Pick yerselves a spot. We're not gonna burn the main house, only the barn and that outbuilding. That'll bring 'em out and we can shoot 'em down."

With trepidation and a definite lack of enthusiasm, Zeke Stokes' meat hunters staked out their horses, then surrounded the ranch house, while Zeke busily gathered brush and hauled an armload to the barn. He stood next to the adobe wall and cursed quietly. How the hell was he supposed to get this pile of mud burning? He moved across the yard to the smokehouse and piled the brush alongside it. Unlike the barn, it was constructed of logs. He got a small handful of kindling and positioned it at the base of the brush and put flint to steel, having to strike it a few times before he got it flaming.

Johanson, Petersen, and the other two men spread out and took up positions at the breaking corral and the remuda corral, and in the brush behind the ranch house. They had just gotten in place when Johanson decided he had had enough of Zeke Stokes and his brothers. He slipped through the brush to Petersen, whom he had formed a friendship with.

"I don't like this," he whispered. "This ain't my fight."

"Nor I," Petersen said quietly.

"Let's hotfoot it back to the camp, take one wagon and a load a' meat, our share, and head for Sacramento City."

"Stokes'll hunt us down."

"Maybe . . . maybe not. I'm going." Johanson set out for his horse, and Petersen followed close behind.

Zeke moved back out of the growing light of the burning brush, content that the smokehouse was going to catch. He licked then used his thumb to wet the front sight of the Hawken he carried, then hunkered down behind a big live oak trunk and glued his attention on the front door of the ranch house.

To his surprise, the sounds of men came from the little smokehouse, not the ranch house. As the flames caught the underside of the small overhang and began to really burn, he heard shouts.

"Help! Help us! Get us outta here!"

The voices were those of his brothers. That damned stupid Mort and Obe were in the smokehouse. The damn fools!

One of the Yocuts was the first to come running out of the ranch house. Zeke laid his sights on him and the big Hawken boomed. The man spun into the dust of the yard and lay unmoving. Zeke, who carried a pistol as well as the Hawken, palmed it, and quickly reloaded the rifle. But his attention kept being distracted by the growing fire as the smokehouse caught, and his brothers began to yell in earnest.

Inside the ranch house, the others were immediately on their feet. Even Ramón managed to grab his old musket and take a position at the window. Gideon pulled himself to a sitting position in his bunk and hefted a pistol. The other Yocuts armed themselves with their bows and the man with the spear and atlatl seated the long weapon in its throwing stick, and they waited.

Clint stood near the darkened doorway, studying the situation.

"Must be Zeke Stokes. He's got the smokehouse burning." Clint edged closer to the doorway. "Stokes!" he yelled out.

"Come on out," a voice rang out of the darkness.

"Your brothers are in the *matanza*."

"Speak the King's English," Zeke snapped.

"That smokehouse has your brothers inside, and they're tied up. You're cooking them alive."

Zeke glanced at the smokehouse and listened to the cries of his brothers. To run into the light of the burning building now would expose him to gunfire from the ranch house. He yelled, "Petersen, Johanson, get over here and open this damned door . . . Obe and Mort are inside. I'll cover ya'll."

But he got no answer, and no one moved from the shadows.

"They was gonna burn in hell anyways," he shouted back to Clint, but his voice had lost some of the edge.

The other three meat hunters listened to this exchange. One of them edged away from his hiding place toward the horses. Before he had gone twenty paces, the other two followed. They were not surprised to find Johanson's and Petersen's horses gone. They too feared Zeke Stokes coming after them . . . so they took his horse. That would slow down any pursuit.

The two narrow windows in the ranch house faced forward, but there was one other way out. The woodbox in the back wall opened both inside and out. Billy hunkered behind his bunk, fully awake now. Clint turned to him.

"Billy, start pulling the firewood out of the box so we can get out through there . . . but be careful. Some of Stokes' men may be around back."

Then Clint turned his attention back to the doorway while Billy and the Yocuts fell to work.

"Give it up, Stokes . . . there's nothing for you here!"

"You got money. I know ya'll sold all those horses."

"We had a bear here and the horses are turned out. They're running free. There's no money here."

Clint talked to keep Stokes busy. Then the jamb of the doorway splintered with the roar of the Hawken again. This time Ramón saw the flash of the big rifle and returned fire.

"Just to the right of the *matanza*," he advised Clint. "Behind the oak."

The front of the oak trunk was now well lighted by the blazing building. Clint positioned himself back away from the doorway where he had a clear view. He laid the revolving breech Colt's down and lined up his shot. As fast as he could fire and work the rotating breech, he snapped off five shots.

Zeke pressed himself against the tree trunk. Must be a dozen of those louts in there, he surmised. Why the hell weren't his other men firing? Why hadn't they done what he commanded and opened the smokehouse door?

His brothers were being burned up.

Zeke faded back away from the trunk, careful to keep the three-foot-wide cover between him and the ranch house doorway until he was well into the darkness, then he ran around out of sight to the breaking corral, where two of his meat hunters had taken up a position.

No one.

He moved on to the remuda corral, then to the adobe walls of the barn. Still no one.

The dirty bastards had left him—run off with their tails between their legs. And cooked his brothers.

He couldn't take a dozen men by himself, he decided quickly, and made his way into the brush after his horse—his stomach queasy with the thought of his brothers and what had been done to them.

It was his hunters' fault. If they hadn't run . . . if they had done what he said and let Mort and Obe out . . . He wanted these damned shirkers dead anyway, so now he would hunt them down and one by one, pick them off. No one could outhunt Zeke Stokes.

He stood in exasperation in the little clearing where the horses had been tied. The bastards had taken his horse! Well, there were horses in the breaking corral. He would go back and fetch one of them.

Clint watched from deep in the doorway, waiting for return fire from behind the oak, but none came. He slipped back to the woodbox as soon as Billy called out that it was clear, and though it was a tight fit, managed to work his way through. Carefully, he pushed up the lid on the outside and studied the scrub oak thicket beyond the clearing as best he could in the darkness. The licking flames were now high above the *matanza* and lit a good portion of the ranch house yard and the thicket beyond. The screams had stopped. The Stokes brothers, at least Mort and Obe, had been hoisted with their own petard.

Clint had not been looking forward to hanging them, and even less to taking them all the way to Stockton or Sacramento City to stand trial, and he had not yet made up his mind about which to do.

Zeke Stokes had solved that problem for him.

Clint sprang from the woodbox and ran into the scrub oaks, then picked his way around to a spot behind the live oak trunk. One of his shots might have hit Zeke, but he doubted it. He studied the spot for a moment, then charged forward. Nothing.

He yelled to the house, "He's gone."

Clint moved back into the darkness again and circled around behind the breaking corral. Nothing. He moved on to the adobe walls of the beginning of the barn. The man, or men, must have left.

"They lit out!" he yelled to the house. The Yocuts poured out; Ramón limped along behind them. At first cautious, they stayed in the shadows, then, confident that the men were gone, filtered into the light.

Zeke Stokes had almost reached the corral, but slid to a stop when he saw a half-dozen figures in the light of the burning smokehouse. Damn, there were probably more of the louts elsewhere. He dropped to one knee and brought the Hawken to his shoulder. That no good Ryan stood in plain sight, clearly back-lit by the burning structure.

Zeke sighted on the man's broad back. His finger tightened on the trigger . . . then he reconsidered. The rest of them would just run him to ground like a coon, and he had more important business. The bastards who had murdered his brothers had to be run down and he had a camp full of meat to haul to Sacramento. Ryan could wait.

He moved back into the scrub oak and began to circle the

house. They would be looking for him, come first light. He needed a horse. He would hide out and wait until he had an opening, then he would steal one of their horses and light a shuck out of there.

For the time being, he would get a good way from the ranch house. Coming to the edge of the tules, he studied them for a moment. A man would be almost impossible to track in there. Without a second thought, Zeke shouldered his way into the tule stand. His boots sucked at the mud for a moment, but he quickly learned to step into the edge of the tules, forcing them down so they became somewhat solid footing. He avoided the deeper bogs.

This would be easy. He would move into the tule thicket and wait until things settled down at the ranch, and he could steal a horse.

But deep in the bog was safest. From time to time he came upon a high spot and could move quickly where it was dry. Finally, he decided he had gone far enough. A lonely scrub oak stood on a rise among the tules, outlined against the starlit sky, and he moved to its shelter and leaned the Hawken against it, kicking the underbrush away so he would have a comfortable place to lie down.

He paused for a moment to think about his brothers . . . poor dumb Obe, even Mort wasn't so bad. Maybe he could get a shot at that son-of-a-bitch Ryan after he got a horse.

He was busily clearing a spot to rest in, when he heard the sound behind him. It was three paces to the Hawken, so he snaked the pistol out of its sheath as he spun to face whoever had tracked him.

"God damn," he managed, as the huge form rose above him out of the tule thicket—its reverberating roar telling Zeke he faced a mortal enemy. The pistol fired, and the bear dropped to all fours, disappearing into the tules.

Zeke stared in amazement. The pistol was no match for a grizzly.

He turned and dove for the Hawken and rolled with it in his hands. But before he could get it positioned, the bear was on him from the side, bursting out of the cover, the darkness—paces from where he had entered the tules. The rifle flew into the tangle with a sweep of the bear's paw.

Zeke scrambled backward on his knees, facing the bear. For a long moment they glared at each other, each of them on all fours.

The bear cut his eyes away to the undergrowth then back at the man.

For a moment, Zeke thought the monster would make for the tules and was going to leave him be. Then, with a great roar, the bear set his hindquarters and lunged forward, his forepaws sweeping like razor-sharp scythes.

Zeke dove to the side and gained his feet, but the tangles of dead tules underfoot snatched at him, and before he could take two steps the bear was on him, smashing him face down into the mud and reed entanglement.

He felt the skin and flesh being torn from his back as the bear's claws raked at him. Then the animal stopped.

Bile rose in Zeke's throat, and he tried not to cough. He couldn't repress it, hacked, and again tried to scramble to his feet to run.

This time he felt the bear's jaw clamp over his thigh. The animal hoisted him and moved through the tules as easily as if it was carrying a rabbit. Zeke bent double and madly beat at the bear with his fists—and it worked. The bear dropped him.

Zeke tried to rise, but the leg wouldn't work. He remembered the Arkansas toothpick and clawed it out of its sheath at his belt.

The bear remained four paces away, watching him.

Zeke held the knife out in front of him.

"Come on, ya beggar. I'll open ya like a satchel."

Twotoes rose slowly on his hind feet and looked down on the miserable creature who he sensed had caused him so much hurt. The smell of this man-animal was the same that had been on the trap that had taken his toes, the same that had bothered him so often when he had been driven from his high mountain home. The same that had caused the pain that worked at his insides like a ball of snakes.

A smell he hated worse than any other.

He flung his head back and roared, but the man didn't turn and run.

Zeke waved the big knife in front of him, its blade flashing in the soft moonlight. He could see where the pistol ball had gouged a deep furrow in the bear's side, a gleam of blood in the night light. Hardly a killing wound, but this bear had turned and run from his pistol shot. This bear wasn't so tough.

"Run, you pig-eyed pile of fat, and I'll hunt you down," Zeke snarled with a tone that denied the flood of fear that racked his guts. With blood pouring down his back and with a leg gnawed to the bone, he was a less than imposing sight.

The bear dropped back to all fours, rocking back and forth in indecision, a quiet rumble deep in his throat.

"Yer the son of a whore," Zeke said, if only for the comfort of hearing his own voice over the low growl of the grizzly. "Run, bear, and I'll have yer hide tacked to the wall before summer's done."

But the bear charged.

Zeke lunged with the knife but a powerful paw sent it reeling into the tules before it bit flesh. Zeke spun and tried to dive into the tules after it. His leg failed him.

This time the bear's jaws slammed with bone-crunching power over the back of Zeke's thick neck.

Twotoes shook the man-animal until it stopped kicking, then dropped it in the mud. Watching it a few moments, he snorted, and rocked back and forth. Finally, when it didn't move again, he scraped tules and mud over it, more from habit than because he wished to protect it from scavengers, snorted again to clear his nostrils of its stench, then ambled off into the tules to find a good mud bog to ease the new wound, and some peace.

"That's the most terrible damn thing I ever saw," Ramón said as the *matanza* burned down to a pile of embers.

"Horrible," Clint said, staring in morbid fascination, his features hardened. "Let's make sure it doesn't happen to us. We're going to post two guards until daylight, then keep one posted until we find out just who this was and where they are—as if I didn't know who. Old Zeke Stokes must have wanted that coffee real bad. I still can't figure why he would cremate his own brothers."

"Some things are just beyond figuring," Ramón said. "I can take the watch till morning."

"What you're gonna take is the bed for a few days, Señor Diego," Clint said. "Limp your arse back in there now. I'll take the rest of the night, what little is left, with Trokhud."

Without argument, Ramón, Billy, and the Yocuts joined Gideon back in the ranch house.

The night passed without further incident.

Fifteen

TWOTOES HAD YET another bullet wound.

This pistol ball had glanced off his ribs, digging a deep gouge but doing no serious damage—but producing again a wound he could not reach to lick. He had killed the man-animal easily, and out of instinct buried it, again protecting his territory. But he would not eat it, for he had no appetite for men.

He wanted the horse, so with the light he headed back through the tules to the place he had left it.

He lay deep in the scrub oak thicket and watched the beehive activity around the ranch. The smell of fire and smoke was everywhere. The gouge in his side bothered him, and he decided the horse was not worth the risk of more contact with the man-animals. As much as he wanted the horse, almost every time he had come into contact with the man-animals, he had paid a heavy price for it. He backed far away from the ranch and turned east.

Soon he had settled into a ground-eating pace.

In the far distance the high country beckoned. If the wound deep in his chest would allow it, in a few days he would be lolling in the bear clover near the thicket of lodgepole pine, in a spot where upon occasion he could look down upon the clouds.

A spot where he had seen the man-animal but once.

Or even higher in the mountains. A spot where he was king of all he surveyed.

. . . .

After determining that the raiders had gone, the men at the ranch house gathered around the *matanza*, coffee cups in hand. They had no appetite for anything else with the happenings of the night still fresh in their minds.

"Let's get them buried," Clint said, not relishing the process and glad he had nothing on his stomach other than coffee.

It was a grisly job, but easily done once they had Mort and Obe, or what was left of them, wrapped in pack canvas and hauled to the top of the scrub oak hill. The Yocuts helped. They also had one of their own to bury—but he would be taken to a sacred place not far from their village on the Tule River. Clint convinced the Yocuts not to leave until he had completed one more task. He also convinced Trokhud, who had won his respect, to select one more man and return to work on the rancho after they finished burying their own—with the incentive that they could own their own rifles and learn to ride horses.

Clint's other task was Gordy Jessup.

Neither Gideon nor Ramón was fit to do anything other than lie around and mend. Gideon could only hobble with one heel badly mauled and his left arm useless in a sling, but he would heal. Ramón was shot through and through, but it seemed a clean wound and had glazed over nicely.

That afternoon, Clint, leading a pack horse, rode out alone to recover what was left of Gordy and bring him back to be buried on the hill overlooking the Rancho Kaweah buildings and corrals. While he was there, and after he had finished the grisly job of rolling the scavenger-ravaged Gordy in a pack canvas and loading him on the pack horse, Clint investigated the stream. When he was satisfied that the stream was a real gold strike, he headed back.

Alone, Clint buried Gordy on the hill, apart from the Stokes boys in a nice spot near a huge live oak that overlooked the rancho. A spot he decided would become the rancho funeral plot. Clint had selected a place of honor, but more for Billy's sake than Gordy's.

While he was gone the Yocuts had tracked the bear into the tules and found the remains of Zeke Stokes. He had joined his brothers on the hill, but not before he had given up the pouches he carried in his belt.

Only after Gordy was buried did Clint fetch Billy. He didn't want the boy to see the gruesome remains of his father. They held a small service over the grave, and that night, a special grace was said before the evening meal. Only Clint and Billy sat at the table; Ramón and Gideon ate in their beds, where Clint insisted they stay.

After they had finished eating, over coffee, Gideon studied Clint from his bunk. "Losin' a smokehouse can't be all that bad, Clint. What's troubling you?"

"That damned grizzly. It's bloody uncomfortable around here with him lurking in the tules ready to make supper out of whoever wanders that way."

"He'll move on," Gideon said.

"Maybe, maybe not. He's already had a taste of horseflesh. I imagine he'll hang around so long as we've got a herd here . . . if we can find the damned horses again."

Ramón leaned up in his bunk. "We will find them much easier this time than the job of catching them in the first place. They will not go far, and many will come with the wave of a nosebag."

"Probably. But come back just to feed that damned bear?" Clint shook his head. "No, I better finish the job the Stokes boys started. In the morning, I'm setting to tracking that brute."

"Then I will go with—" Ramón began.

"The hell you will," Clint snapped uncharacteristically. "You and Gideon will stay right there in those bunks. Billy can watch over you two, can't you, Billy?"

"Yes, sir," Billy said.

"If you two don't get well, who the devil is going to finish the barn?" Clint said, smiling again.

"He is *oso diablo*," Ramón cautioned.

"He's no devil bear, just an old griz carrying a lot of the Stokes brothers' lead, probably sick as hell, and understandably looking for an easy meal . . . and penned-up horses are one. It's just too damn bad that he was hurt bad enough to have to go after that

Yocuts boy. Now I've got to hunt him down . . . and we'll have a big rug to throw in front of the fire come winter."

"Poco tiempo," Ramón offered. "Give him a little time and maybe he will leave on his own."

"I don't think we can afford to give him time. It's a problem I've got to solve so we can get back to work in peace."

"It is dangerous, amigo. Three men have been hunting him, skilled bear hunters. You should wait."

"No waiting, we've got work to do as soon as you two loafers are mended," Clint said kiddingly.

Clint looked at his two friends, but neither of them was smiling.

"Vaya con Dios, El Lazo," Ramón said.

The meat hunters had returned to camp to find their barrels broken and the meat, what wasn't eaten, scattered and being fed upon by a host of scavengers.

A family of black bears, a sow and her unusual array of three yearling cubs, had managed to destroy two months' work—and had driven off the remaining stock. The meat hunters salvaged a few hides, harnessed up four of the five riding horses, and hauled out of there with the empty wagons. The wagons and hides could be sold and the men would at least make wages.

Before dawn, Clint had Diablo saddled and a pack horse loaded.

He was literally loaded for bear.

His .50 caliber Hawken rode in a saddle boot on one side of the saddle, his revolving .36 caliber Colt's rifle on the other. One .36 caliber Navy Colt's rode on his hip and another was jammed into a saddle holster.

Even though only a single shot, the big-bore Hawken was the only weapon for a full-grown, seven-hundred-pound boar grizzly. And this big griz had experience with man and guns—he would be no easy hunt.

Billy walked from the ranch house with Smiley trailing close behind, still limping.

"You ought to take Smiley with you, Mr. Ryan," Billy offered.

"I would, Billy me lad, if he was fit. But this ol' griz may run or he may turn and fight, and Smiley is fit for neither. But it's kind of you to offer."

"I could go with you. Ramón and Gideon can—"

"I need you here, Billy. You're the only one left who's a hundred percent. No, you take care of the ranch and those two worthless bedbugs in there."

Billy laughed, then his face went pale.

"What's the matter, boy?" Clint asked as he swung up easily into the saddle.

"I just don't . . . ," he said quietly, then flushed and turned away.

"What's the matter, boy? Spit it out."

"Be careful," Billy muttered, running for the house, with Smiley limping along behind him. He paused just before he entered the ranch house door and yelled back at Clint, "Be really careful."

"Nothing will happen to this old sailor." Clint waved, and touched Diablo gently with the spurs.

Billy ran on into the house without turning back, but as he rode out, Clint saw him peeking from the window. Clint waved, but Billy disappeared from sight.

It didn't take long to pick up the grizzly's tracks. Clint made a circle, followed the tule line, and soon found where the big animal had left its confines. The trail led back to within forty yards of the house, where the bear had bedded down for a while. It gave Clint a chill to realize that the bear had been watching the rancho.

It also steeled his resolve. This bear was a man-killer and must be brought down.

While tracking, he also found the hoof prints of several shod horses who had accompanied Zeke Stokes to Rancho Kaweah. All of them had ridden out, and the same way he was traveling, east, upriver. Not only must he be on the lookout for the bear, but he must now, he realized, watch out for the meat hunters. So far they had proved to be the worst of enemies.

Past the rancho, the griz trail made a beeline back to the deep canyon where Clint had the logging camp. Clint pushed the horses hard, reining up only twice to track the bear on foot where a rock shelf pushed out of the hills to the riverside. But the bear, Clint decided, was determined, and had a destination in mind—if bears did such things.

By the end of the day Clint still followed a clear trail upriver. He had crossed the trail of the meat hunters several times, but the bear's prints were over them, so they must have ridden out ahead of the big boar. Clint wondered if perhaps the bear wasn't trailing the meat hunters. That would be a switch.

He reached his former campsite where the felled lodgepole pine still rested, ready to begin a float downriver, then passed the remnants of the hunters' camp. What a mess it was. They were gone, and most of their work lay in ruin and stench. He decided the hunters must have rolled out on the north side of the river, for he had followed the south side for most of the way and not seen the wagon tracks until he was almost upon their campsite.

He hoped they weren't headed back to Rancho Kaweah. It was a possibility, but one he hoped was remote. Without their leader, Zeke Stokes, he doubted if they had any more intentions toward Rancho Kaweah.

He made camp on a rock shelf near the river, well upstream from the hunters' camp, at the base of the mountain, below the spot where much higher on the mountainside the great rock dome rose almost straight up.

He built a bigger fire than he needed, and still slept fitfully. It was too bad he couldn't have brought Smiley along; he could have served as watch dog, and Clint would have slept much better.

The next morning, Clint got his wish about climbing the canyon side. The bear's trail turned up, and the animal wasn't bashful about climbing. Clint had to work the horses back and forth in long switchbacks, watching for the animal's trail as he crossed it.

At first, he passed through thickets of sandpaper oak. The smallish trees at times completely blocked his passage, but showed tunnels of game trails that allowed the shorter deer, and the bear when on all fours, to pass. An occasional brush rabbit burst from the undergrowth, sometimes close enough to the palomino to make him dance and sidestep on the trail. Ground squirrels sat up near holes or rock piles and studied him, then scampered to the safety of their dens as they decided he was too near. The shadows of redtail hawks and an occasional golden eagle flickered across the trail, causing Clint to glance up and admire their silent glide, and causing the squirrels to duck for cover. Patiently, they circled the thickest stands and picked up the bear's trail on the upper side. He could hear, more than see, deer moving out of the thickets ahead of him, scolded by ravens, mockingbirds, and meadowlarks. Twice Clint reached for the Hawken, startled as coveys of quail exploded from the hillside in his path, then laughed at himself and relaxed as he watched them set their wings and glide away down the canyon to safety.

In the few openings where the chaparral gave way to sunlit meadows, buttercups, yellow violets, fiddleneck, and poppies blazed the steep meadows with color.

Redbud and flannel brush surrounded escarpments of rock slides alive with golden-mantle ground squirrels and Merriam chipmunks, where nodding fairy lanterns with petals like pink satin curved together under sepals of maroon and fought to gain root-hold among the sharp-edged piles, contrasting with the inhospitable blue granite which served as their tenuous home. A rattler buzzed in the rocks, but far enough away that the steady horse only glanced up and pointed his ears, then continued. Crossing these rocks required great concentration on the part of the big palomino, and Clint could do nothing but let him carefully pick his own way, then work to find the bear's trail on the far side of the rock falls.

Finally, the scrub oak gave way to blue and white oak, more sparsely scattered, then golden-cup oaks billowing out of the canyon walls like puffs of brown-green clouds. The going was easier in the sparse stands of trees, but tougher as it became ever steeper, and he had to skirt manzanita, bright with waxy green leaf and red bark. An occasional buckeye, toyon, or California bay rose among the oaks offering brilliant new green to contrast with the simple gray-green of the lower vegetation, and chickaree squirrels scampered among their branches, amazing Clint with their ability to run almost straight down a thick tree trunk. They too scolded him with sharp barks for intruding on their territory.

Clint reined up in a shady ravine with a trickle of water, where a pair of sycamores had found roothold, and dismounted to let the big palomino blow and nuzzle the moss aside in a shallow pond to drink. He sat on a rock and admired its thick coverlet of pipevine, with maroon flowers curved like its namesake and proving to be an inviting death for insects which crawled inside only to be trapped by tiny hairs pointing downward. A Scott's Oriole, bright lemon underbelly contrasting with black head, white-striped-black wings and tail, moved among the flowers, stealing the captured insects then pausing to break the silence with a series of rising and falling flute-like notes. Disturbed by Clint and the horse, his song became a harsh chuck-chuck and he retreated to the nearby oaks.

Each time he allowed himself to be enchanted by the changing cover and wildlife, Clint shook himself back to reality—and the bear.

He remounted and plodded onward, ever climbing.

The oaks gave way to incense cedars, yellow pine, and white fir in hundred-foot-wide tables where the steep slope eased. The trees formed a great green wall and he had to carefully plot his crossing —always aware the bear might have backtracked and be waiting.

Finally, after hours of this, he reached the bottom of the granite dome, where the bear had turned and followed the base of the rock. At times Clint rode with his shoulder almost against the vertical rock wall; at times he had to skirt a rubble escarpment. Now he could look down on the gliding redtail hawks and golden eagles below. Level with his eye were Clark's nutcrackers in the very tops of the firs and pines that rose from the steep canyon side below him, their cheek-pouches packed with nuts, surveying the trees below for even more. An occasional scrub or Steller's jay sassed the bigger birds with a loud jree jree, unsuccessfully trying to rout them from their treetop perch.

Now the trail was almost impossible to follow. Many times he had to dismount and go afoot up the escarpment to find the bear's tracks, or claw marks, or broken twigs and branches where the bear had passed through the occasional brush in the almost barren rock face.

The going was tough for Clint, carrying the heavy Hawken, the Colt's pistol strapped on his side, the Colt's revolving breech rifle in reserve in its saddle boot—always aware of the bear's possible ambush. With each sound he responded; each pile of brush or rock might hide an ambushing, wounded, seven-hundred-pound killer.

He often had to skirt thick heavy-branched manzanita thickets, where the bear had gone through, and pick up the trail on the other side.

But always he climbed.

And now the granite dome was at his side. By day's end he could see what he thought was the canyon rim above him, but even from there the dome continued to rise high above. The trees on the top, still a thousand feet over him, seemed much taller than the puzzle bark ponderosa pine trees he decided to camp among—and they rose over a hundred feet in height. A few western red cedars also rose majestically nearby, which he made note of, for he needed one for shingles. He hoped the bear stayed out of the cedars, for there it was so thick he could see only for a few feet. He could imagine nothing more treacherous than hunting the bear there.

He made a dry camp on the steep canyon side, walked to the cedars, where a trickle of water began its fall down the escarpment, and filled his canteen and watered Diablo. There he was treated to a pair of blue grouse in a clearing below the stand of cedar. The male, perched on a fallen pine log above the plainer female, strutted, spread his tail feathers wide, and boomed his mating call—a sound Clint was glad he knew the origin of—by inflating and deflating purple feathered pouches on each side of his neck. But his serenade seemed unsuccessful, as the female ignored him and retreated to a nearby pine to fill her beak with pine needles.

Just before dark Clint walked to a rock outcropping and watched the sunset far across the Ton Tache Valley. At least two thousand feet below, the distance he and the horses had traversed that day, he could see the Kaweah River winding its way down the canyon among bright green new growth buckeye and gray-green scrub oak to the tules in the valley. A flock of two dozen band-tailed pigeons winged at breakneck speed below him, the swoosh of their wings testifying they would find a safe perch well before the increasing darkness fell to black. He could not see the lumber camp or the old meat hunters' camp, but just as the sun painted the western sky in brilliant oranges and yellows, he thought, just for a moment, that he could see a tendril of smoke where he thought Rancho Kaweah must lie. He glanced into the growing shadows of the deep forest above and up the side of the sheer granite edifice, out at the immense country which fell away before him, and felt very small.

Again, he built a much bigger fire than he needed.

His sleep was broken many times by the sounds of night creatures, and a pair of squabbling raccoons sent him scrambling for the Hawken once, only to laugh at himself again. Morning came without incident, and the cold of the high altitude kept him in the bedroll for a little longer than he might have stayed in the valley below.

After being in the saddle for only a few minutes, he considered abandoning the horses and letting them find their own way back to the rancho. He decided to let the pack horse go. He dismounted on the steep mountainside and repacked a few provisions in his saddlebags, hoisted the pack high up off the ground with a reata thrown over a high ponderosa pine branch, and slapped the pack horse on the rump.

Then he and Diablo began the real climb, Clint leading the big palomino. There was no tracking the bear here; he would have to pick up the trail again on the top of the mountain. The terrain was almost vertical, any steeper and they could not have gone on, but it lay sparse of timber and the sun felt good on his shoulders. He was more worried about the rattlers than the bear in this open country, for many times the side hill was so steep he was face to face with ledges. Being struck in the face or neck by a snake was not his idea of a good introduction to the high country, and he could see their track where they had slithered across the trail in their night hunt. Finally, after Clint had climbed all morning, many times sliding back almost as far as he moved upward, the slope began to ease.

Clint took a breather, letting Diablo graze on a patch of grass. They stood at the edge of a stand of golden oak which gave way to tall ponderosa pine. The pines, with their distinctive puzzle bark, rose well over a hundred feet in the air; many were four feet in diameter. Clint paused in the middle of the grove to admire them, then began his quest again. He swept back and forth on the slope until, as he was sure he would, he picked up the distinctive track of the two-toed grizzly again.

Still the animal's trail pushed upward.

The forest undergrowth gave way to ferns, the cover overhead so thick that the damp mossy forest floor got no light. Clint was busily tracking when he glanced up, then reined up.

He gasped, then, for a moment, held his breath.

In front of him was the largest living thing he had ever seen. A tree. But to call it merely that was like calling the mountain of granite he had ridden around a rock.

This tree was ten paces across. Its lower limbs did not begin until a distance up its trunk that was halfway up the tallest ponderosa—and the first limb's diameter was as great as the trunks of its neighboring pines.

Tremors of awe traversed Clint's back; not a chill of fear, but one of utter awe—and it was added to by the absolute silence of the place. So quiet it was, he wondered if he could hear the sap flow in the giant tree. He slipped from the saddle and moved forward on foot, forgetting even the Hawken. The old monster tree had been scarred with fire—many fires, Clint guessed.

He sat quietly and crossed his legs and stared, with maidenhair and sword ferns surrounding him. He studied the tree, almost too much in awe to approach it—to believe it. Was it a freak of nature? No, he decided, as he looked deeper into the dark forest and made out others.

Slowly he rose to his feet and moved forward until he could reach out and touch it. Its reddish brown trunk was fibrous, fluted in great vertical ravines, almost mimicking a steep mountain or cliff side as it rose from the nearly barren ground beneath it.

"My God," Clint finally said aloud; then his attention was drawn to Diablo, who snorted in reply. The big horse was not looking at Clint, but rather beyond him, around the giant tree, at something Clint could not see.

This time the chill that traversed his backbone was one of fear. In his excitement, he had left the Hawken in its boot on Diablo.

He rested his hand on the butt of the Navy Colt's on his hip and began moving to the big horse. Diablo snorted again and backed away. Clint studied the shadows of the forest and made out the shape of the bear. It watched him, nonmenacing, silent, unmoving. Clint could not see the animal's eyes but could feel them on him. A presence almost as powerful as the formidable tree.

"Stand, Diablo," Clint commanded, and the big horse shook his head nervously, but let Clint approach. He slipped the Hawken from the saddle boot and spun to face the spot where he had seen the bear, ratcheting back the hammer in the same motion, but the animal had slipped into the darkness among the giant trees.

Clint stood quietly listening. The silence of the forest was more imposing than that of a cathedral. Clint had visited many in South America and Mexico in his travels as a sailor, but none of man's works compared with this—God's own. God's own cathedral, that's what this place was.

The majesty of the place overwhelmed him, almost making him forget the bear, then he shook it off and mounted, urging Diablo forward to pick up the trail of the grizzly again.

For hours they moved quietly, softly, through the majestic trees. At one time they reined up amid more than a hundred, each reaching for the heavens—how high? Clint knew he must find a hillside where he could gauge the height of the incredible trees—not that anyone would believe him.

He came upon one felled by time, he supposed. He dismounted and paced along it, but this time remembered to carry the Hawken. Seventy-two paces. He didn't believe it, and paced back the other way. Two hundred and sixteen feet, and he was sure it wasn't the largest among them. He climbed to the top of the trunk and walked it from one end to the other, then climbed down and went to its base, which was hollow. Given a few touches of remodeling, it would have made a respectable house.

"My God," he repeated reverently. He mounted Diablo again, and reluctantly continued his hunt.

Nothing could smell as fresh and clean as the forest he rode through. It cleansed his nostrils of the stench of the last few days. It cleansed his soul of the killing he had seen.

The bear began following a trickle of water lined by fresh shoots of grass and brilliant green moss, winding its way between the giant trees. It was hard for Clint to track, for he continually found himself staring up at the majesty overhead.

The trickle grew, and the forest thinned until Clint spotted the brilliant green of a sunlit meadow in the distance amid the giant tree trunks.

Instinctively, he dismounted. He pulled the Hawken, left the Colt's rifle in its boot, but pulled the second Navy Colt's and stuffed it in his belt. He did not want anything to happen to the palomino, so this time he slipped the bridle off the horse and let it fall among the ferns.

Then he moved forward. He had not seen the grizzly, but somehow knew the huge animal would be in the meadow ahead.

Clint tested the wind. It was difficult to do in among the big trees, which seemed to have their own wind currents moving in and out of the massive trunks, but, satisfied that it was as much in his favor as the bear's, he moved forward.

Clint placed each foot carefully. Not a sound must betray his presence.

A few small lodgepoles nestled in the sunlight at the edge of the meadow, and Clint worked his way into their cover. The trickle had become a streamlet, and it wound into the meadow. Deep with grass and skunk cabbage, the open spot stretched for over two hundred paces and more than fifty wide. It was bracketed on all sides by the magnificent giant trees, and blanketed with lush green highlighted by brilliant wild flowers. Clint settled among the lodgepoles and studied the pastoral scene.

The beauty of it almost took his breath away.

He was jolted back to reality as he caught the movement of the bear's huge back. He must have been in a cut where the stream had worked a ravine in the soft meadow floor. The bear rose on his hind feet and whiffed and snorted, then ambled up and out of the ravine into the meadow grass.

Ever so softly, Clint eased the hammer back on the Hawken. The bear paused and tested the air, but as Clint had surmised, it was with him. Reassured, the bear turned his attention to the lush growth.

Clint brought the heavy rifle to his shoulder and sighted on the massive chest of the grizzly, just where he thought the animal's heart should be, but the bear dropped to all fours and rolled in the grass like a playful dog—as Clint had seen Smiley do so many times.

He lowered the rifle, waiting until the bear stopped moving. He wanted the one shot to be a killing one.

The bear came back to all fours and began feeding on a patch of owl's clover, quietly browsing. Again Clint brought the rifle to his shoulder, but the animal's haunches were to him, not a good angle.

The bear dropped to his hindquarters, sitting like a man in the grass. It was the shot Clint wanted. The bear's wide chest faced him.

Clint snapped the rifle up, and drew a bead on the heart spot, his finger tightened on the trigger, and the bear yawned. A wide gaping yawn of pure contentment.

Clint hesitated. The bear again moved, this time curling up like a cub in the meadow grass, scratching his side against the meadow floor; then he stretched and laid his massive head on his paws.

Even from the distance, Clint could make out the many scars covering the bear.

The rifle felt suddenly heavy.

"Damn you," Clint groused quietly, "why don't you roar at me and show those godawful fangs?"

But the bear closed his eyes and seemed to sleep. He rested at an angle that would be an easy shot, unmoving. One hundred and twenty paces, Clint estimated, testing the wind again. *I could hit him in the eye at this distance, if I wanted to,* Clint thought as he jammed the rifle against his shoulder. *A heart shot, make it a heart shot*—but he let the muzzle drop again.

But I don't want to.

Not here, not in this place.

This was the bear's spot much more than his own.

He was the interloper here, not the grizzly.

Clint turned and quietly made his way out of the lodgepole pines back to where Diablo grazed. He rebridled the big horse and mounted. He glanced back over his shoulder, hoping to catch one more glimpse of the majestic bear. The bear was at home here, driven from here by the hunters. Clint had no business here, certainly no killing business. Not here, not among these trees, this cathedral.

But the bear was nowhere in sight.

He started to urge the stallion forward, then realized the wind had changed. It was in his face, and a ripple of fear traversed his backbone. Had he been foolish, thinking he could merely walk away from this? He had been the hunter; was he now the hunted? There was no way the bear had not caught his scent, with the wind in his face.

Suddenly his every sense was at its peak. His eyes moved from shadow to shadow, his hearing picked up the slightest ruffle of fern. The big stallion snorted his displeasure and his ears focused forward. Clint strained to see into the shadows ahead of them.

Had the bear circled around?

He decided he would not fall for that trap. With Hawken in hand, Clint reined back to the meadow and rode out to the spot where the bear had been, careful, as the deep cut of the ravine in the meadow's soft bottom offered many hiding places, even for the huge griz.

He could clearly see where the bear had clambered out of the cut and had moved, at a run, across the soft bottom, disturbing the grass and leveling a number of tall stalks of skunk cabbage. The bear had left with a purpose.

"Damn your dumb sentimental hide," Clint cursed himself in a soft whisper. "You had him dead to rights. Dead to rights." *Don't make that mistake again.*

Now he had to track again, and the bear definitely knew he was there. The bear would run, but circle and wait. Clint had hunted the big grizzlies many times near Santa Barbara with Ramón and his friends a few years before. One time even when the vaqueros hunted with their reatas—greased with tallow so the bear could not pull a roper into claw and fang range—and six of them, Clint included, had roped and captured a big boar for a bull and bear fight. He knew the animal's habits.

Bad habits, for the hunter.

Constantly panning his gaze from side to side, Clint let Diablo pick his way along the bear's path, guiding the horse with his knees. The open but shaded, ominously silent space beneath the big trees offered little cover for the bear—except for the massive trunks themselves. The bear, if cunning enough, and Clint knew they could be, could move around one of the massive trunks, keeping the redwood between him and the rider, and charge from behind after the rider had passed. Clint decided he must depend upon the senses of the big stallion. He would smell or hear the bear long before Clint would see him.

Still, he made sure the horse stayed centered between the big trunks, which were almost always thirty or forty feet apart, and could not help but continue to glance over his shoulder as they passed through the grove.

Finally, the redwoods gave way to a deep manzanita thicket over a hundred feet through, many of the shrubs as high as the big horse. Clint studied the bear's trail where it entered the thicket, and Diablo's nervous prance convinced him the bear was there, inside, waiting.

The mountain dropped away on the far distant side of the mass of waxy-green leafed shrubs, but rose above it off to Clint's left, where a higher outcropping of granite could be scaled. *From there, I can see almost anywhere in the mass of chaparral,* Clint decided. He moved around the thicket, carefully staying away from spots he could not easily see into.

He dismounted, Hawken in hand, thinking he would climb the granite outcropping, but Diablo suddenly sat back, almost dragging Clint off his feet.

"Easy, boy," Clint said, glancing nervously over his shoulder. He calmed the horse and pulled the bridle away, so the animal had a chance to move freely if need be. Then Diablo reared, and Clint spun to see the reason just when the bear roared. The animal rose to its full height on the outcropping, ten feet above Clint, who snapped the rifle to his shoulder and fired.

The big slug took the bear midchest and knocked him backward, but the animal recovered as quickly and on all fours sprang off the ledge—three quarters of a ton hurtling down on Clint.

The Colt's was in his hand, but he dove to the side to avoid the plunging bear, who hit the ground and stumbled. Clint got off another shot as he backpedaled, knowing he hit the bear, but the animal came on, spinning and charging, spittle and blood flinging from his snarling mouth.

Clint, his back to the granite outcropping, fanned the Colt's, getting off three more quick shots, but the bear came on. Then the big griz rolled to the side, and it was the horse pounding at him with his forefeet that had caused the distraction. The bear rose on his hind feet to meet the new threat. Diablo, eyes flared, teeth bared, spun, giving the bear both rear hooves with a resounding thump to the center of the animal's chest. The bear rolled backward into the manzanita from the ferocity of the horse's kick.

Clint fired twice more, knowing he was hitting the bear, then scrambled to the horse. He had to get the other Colt's pistol or the rifle. He was out of shots.

But the horse reared and sidestepped, his eyes on the bear, who had recovered and stood among the manzanita.

He roared loud enough to shake the nearby redwoods, and

Clint turned to face the animal, which bled from a number of wounds.

The bear, on all fours, seemed to waiver a moment. Blood flowed from his mouth, bright foamy lung blood.

"Die, bear!" Clint yelled, hoping the horse would calm enough for him to lunge for the rifle, but the stallion stayed out of reach, his eyes wide with fear, facing the bear. But he didn't run; he was a fighter.

The bear charged again, slower this time. Clint dove to the side, rolled on his back, scooting away. The bear rose again on his hind legs and stumbled forward, his forelegs flailing the air, his head flinging blood. With a mighty effort, he lunged.

Clint tried to spring away, but the bear was on him, his massive weight pinning him, suffocating him.

Then he realized the bear wasn't moving, it was dead weight that pinned him. For a long moment, he lay there, until he realized he had no one to help him.

With a gargantuan series of efforts, he managed to squeeze out, an inch at a time, from under the bear's weight.

Diablo neighed shrilly, but Clint could only sigh. He got to his feet, only to collapse beside the fallen grizzly, not knowing whether to laugh or cry, so he did neither.

He managed to gasp, "I guess it had to be, bear. You or me, and to tell you the truth, I'm damned glad it was you."

It was the better part of an hour before his blood stopped racing, and he got to his feet and began the all-day chore of skinning the big bear. Before the task was done, he counted fourteen wounds, seven old and seven new. The Hawken slug had exploded the bear's heart and the upper right lung, and still the animal had come on. Four of the Colt's pistol shots had been chest shots, and still the bear had come.

What an animal. What a waste, that he could not have let this majestic beast live, live here where he belonged, and where Clint felt the intruder.

Clint camped there that night, and with a hunter's ritual, roasted and ate a chunk of the grizzly's loin. The rest of the huge beast would go to the scavengers, return to the earth. Dust to dust.

The next morning, Clint walked beside the palomino, who carried the rest of their supplies and over a hundred pounds of bear skin and head. They started home.

It would be a long hard trek, but it was downhill all the way.

He didn't say a word to Gideon and Ramón about the giant trees —they would think the bear had swatted him in the head and knocked his senses loose. He didn't have to say much about the bear; the huge skin was testimony enough, and he had no urge to crow about the killing. He decided he would take them to see the trees when they were adequately healed, and when the work on the ranch was done.

Trokhud and one of his braves had come to the ranch, bringing their women with them, and Clint had instructed them to build substantial huts in the sycamore grove. The Yocuts chief looked with reverence on the bear skin, and with his eyes, thanked Clint for the revenge taken for the death of his son. The Indians helped him tan the hide and work on the barn while his other friends mended.

A week after returning to the ranch, Clint walked from the house to find Billy staring dejectedly at the hill where his father was buried; the track of a tear marked his cheek.

"What's the matter, Billy boy?" Clint asked.

"Nothing," Billy said, glancing over his shoulder.

Clint moved alongside him and laid a hand on his shoulder. "You've got a big year in front of you, Billy."

"How's that?" Billy asked.

"As soon as we get the Yocuts riding, we'll round up the horses."

"Good, then I can keep on training Tache. Will Ramón be able to help?"

"You couldn't keep that vaquero down if there's a horse to train. But you're gonna have bigger fish to fry."

"How so?"

"School, Billy. Your father and I talked about your going to school, and now you can do it."

"There's no school around here, and besides, Pa said it cost a lot of money to go to school."

"You've got a lot of money, Billy me lad."

"I don't have a penny, Mr. Ryan."

"The devil you don't. You've got the gold your pa found, and a gold-filled canyon. As soon as we get those horses rounded up, the barn built, and the smokehouse rebuilt, we're gonna go up and pan you out some more to add to the stake you've already got. Then while you're at school, Ramón and Gideon and I will go up once in a while and pan you out a little. How about half for us for the work, and half for you, since your pa made the find?"

"That sounds fair, but do I have to go to school?"

"You're a man of means, Billy Jessup, a man of means, and if you mean to keep any of it, you'll need to be able to do your sums and cipher. Besides, going to the Sandwich Islands will be a real adventure."

"The Sandwich Islands?"

"The missionaries there have a fine school, and all the Californios have been sending their sons there for years. You'll get the very best education."

"But I'll have to leave Tache," Billy said, his brow furrowed. "And Smiley, what about Smiley?"

"That little horse will do fine on a month-long voyage. You don't have to leave him, he'll go with you. Besides, if he's along, then you might not forget your friends here at Rancho Kaweah. I'd like it if you left Smiley here, but that's up to you. You can take him along if the school approves. We'll write them and find out if you like."

Billy dropped his eyes and kicked a clod. He spoke without looking up. "I'll go, but I want to come back here. This is my home, and Tache's."

"As long as I've got a fire, you've got a spot by it, Billy boy. Let's go saddle up and see if you and I can find some horse sign. I'll just bet I know where those cayuses have run off to."

As they rode out, Billy began to hum the tune Clint had taught him, and before long, they had changed the verse, and were singing loudly.

Hey, it's goodbye Muirsin Durkin
I'm sick and tired of workin'
No more I'll pick the Brady's
No longer I'll be poor.

As sure as my name is Billy
I'm off to the Sandwich country
'Stead of pickin' Brady's
I'll be pickin' lumps of gold

I said goodbye to Shamus
And soon I'll be famous
I'll know readin' and writin'
There'll be no more fightin'

Hey, its goodbye Muirsin Durkin
I'm sick and tired of workin'
No more I'll pick . . .

Author's Note

Like other John Clinton Ryan novels, *Shadow of the Grizzly* has more than one hero and more than one villain.

In this novel California herself is some of each.

The gold rush began the inevitable transition of California as a whole, but no area was finally more affected than her great Central Valley, known to the Indians as the Ton Tache, and later to the Spanish, and even later the Anglo, as the San Joaquin Valley. The great rift between the Coast Range and the Sierra Nevada mountains is the largest flat area in the United States west of the Rocky Mountains—and in the center of it, Ton Tache Lake, later known as Tulare Lake, was the largest body of water west of the Great Lakes, larger even than the Great Salt Lake or Tahoe. It is only a memory now, its waters diverted, its rich bottom soil supporting great cotton and vegetable ranches.

Precipitation in the three-hundred-mile-long valley varies from only seven inches of annual rainfall in the south to thirty in the north. In 1854 that rainfall and the snow melt from the Sierra Nevada mountains (Snowfall Mountains in Spanish) roiled uncontrolled into the valley.

Today it is mostly a quilt pattern of square and rectangular plots of farmland laced with asphalt roads and ringed with fences and power lines; in the 1800s it had a maze of piedmont hills on its borders, and tree-and-tule-lined rivers and sloughs in the valley bottom. Valley waterways bordered a puzzle of bunchgrass-and-deer-brush-covered islands. Not even a rider could cross the valley until much later, unless he risked quicksand making him and his horse permanent residents. Cattle herds and wagon roads stayed far away from the marsh, sticking to the drier piedmont.

Then, borders of the major and minor waterways stood jungle-like where cottonwood, willow, sycamore, box elder, black walnut, bay, and stately valley oak were strung with wild grape and clematis hanging in green curtains, or patched with mistletoe. Dense berry vines, wild rose snarls, poison oak patches, and stinging nettle discouraged casual passage below—even punished its attempt. Where water courses slowed or straightened, seeking the shortest route, they left oxbow bogs in place of the earlier bed, and tules and cattails thrived. Water courses in the valley bottom created prairie islands. On the west slope of the valley (in the much drier rainshadow lee side of the coast range), the Kansas of California predominated—and great prairies of bunchgrass nurtured elk, wild horse, deer, and antelope. Even in those dry savannas, winter-fed vernal rainfall pools slowly receded to welcome encroaching summer, leaving concentric rings of wild flowers, garlands of beauty that changed almost weekly. And for much of the spring and early summer the whole vista, including the backdrop of hills, became a fiesta of wild flower color.

But the tule-rimmed bottom wetlands ruled the valley, and millions of birds thrived. There the great condor—the few remaining confined now to the ornithologist's cage—and turkey vulture circled over all. Below, with watchful immobility, the great blue heron stood among: whistling swans; Canada, white-fronted, and snow geese; and mallard, gadwall, redhead, ruddie, widgeon, and teal ducks. And the waders were everywhere. Black-crowned night and green herons, greater yellowlegs, avocets, stilts, sandpipers, long-billed curlews, white-faced ibis, and egrets roamed the mud banks and shallow water.

Bald and golden eagles; Cooper's, red-tailed, and red-shouldered hawks; and white-tailed kites ruled the day sky; and great horned and long-eared owls the night.

Below the surface of the water courses, life teemed as well:

perch, bass, salmon, carp, lampreys, squawhead, bluegill, and cray-fish shared the water with bullfrogs, which climbed to the mud banks and had to share those with tiger and California salaman-ders, spadefoot and western toads, and a dozen varieties of snakes.

The golden or bank beaver dug his dens in the shorelines, ignor-ing the muskrats and mink and the den-building habits of his mountain counterpart. Coyote, bobcat, gray fox, striped skunk, badger, and wolf sought the nests of birds for young and eggs. Harvest and deer mice, moles, and dusky-footed woodrats ran or burrowed along the surface near the water, while kangaroo rats hopped there, all taking insects, grubs, or seeds.

And all life, even the black bear, paid homage to the grizzly, who ruled over all until the coming of man—and without his guns, man, too, would have yielded.

It is said that no environment has been more drastically changed in such a short period as has the San Joaquin Valley.

The valley then was a cornucopia of wildlife, but its rich bottom land beckoned men. Now, drained and plowed, surveyed and county-recorded, spotted with irrigation pumps and standpipes and fertilizer and pesticide tanks, it provides half the nation's fruit and vegetables. Again a cornucopia in its own progressive way—or regressive way, depending upon your point of view.

This year, for the first time ever, the author relented to "prog-ress," and fished the concrete-lined canal of the central valley wa-ter project where striped bass have, like the author, acclimated. Somehow, without the bordering tules and contingency of red-wing blackbirds, it lacked.

But there, beside the canal, before the land again conceded to plowed fields, lay a lonely piece of virgin valley—not more than ten acres, but a tiny, overlooked, sage-covered remnant of the past.

With a friend, the concrete-byway bass being unwilling to sur-render, I walked there—two hundred years earlier in spirit—and studied this chunk of natural California as I had done many times in many places as a boy, wandering the valley before it gave up almost completely to progress. With the same enthusiasm as I had as a seven-year-old, I pried open the perfectly camouflaged airtight lids to the dens of trapdoor spiders.

As my eyes adjusted to something other than traffic lights and neon signs, my walk yielded two tiny remembrances of that better time, and better times before. A $^{3}/_{8}$-inch olivella shell that had been carefully drilled so it could join others on a bead necklace was the first. Then a beautifully sculptured obsidian arrowhead, not more than $^{5}/_{8}$ of an inch in length, lay exposed by recent rains.

I had been touched by a Yocuts squaw, then a Yocuts brave.

As I rolled his tiny artwork over and over in my hand—as the Yocuts brave had once proudly done—the concrete canal and overhead lines and plowed fields seemed to disappear, and the cry of the whistling swan, bugle of the bull elk, and roar of the grizzly ruled the land again. A hunter-gatherer stood where I stood, gathering net hanging from his shoulder, bow in hand, tiny-headed arrow notched, stalking a covey of valley quail or a brush rabbit.

Suddenly the automatic pumps on a nearby canal lift station roared the twentieth century to life. I raised my eyes from the powdery valley floor and found the sky occluded with smog and crisscrossed with jet contrails.

But I still have his arrowhead, and her tiny adornment. And I appreciate his finely wrought pagan sculpture—a labor not only of love but of survival for that long-ago Yocuts—as much as I might appreciate a less necessary Rodin work of sculptured marble, or, maybe more appropriately, a Remington or Russell bronze.

And I, like many, long for a time when the land was hers and his, and above all, its own.

ABOUT THE AUTHOR

Larry Jay Martin writes of Old California with an excitement and historical accuracy that few could match. He is the author of four previous El Lazo novels, as well as his historical epic, *Rush to Destiny*, a novelization of the life of Edward Fitzgerald Beale. Larry Jay Martin lives in Bakersfield, California, with his wife Kat, a bestselling romance novelist.